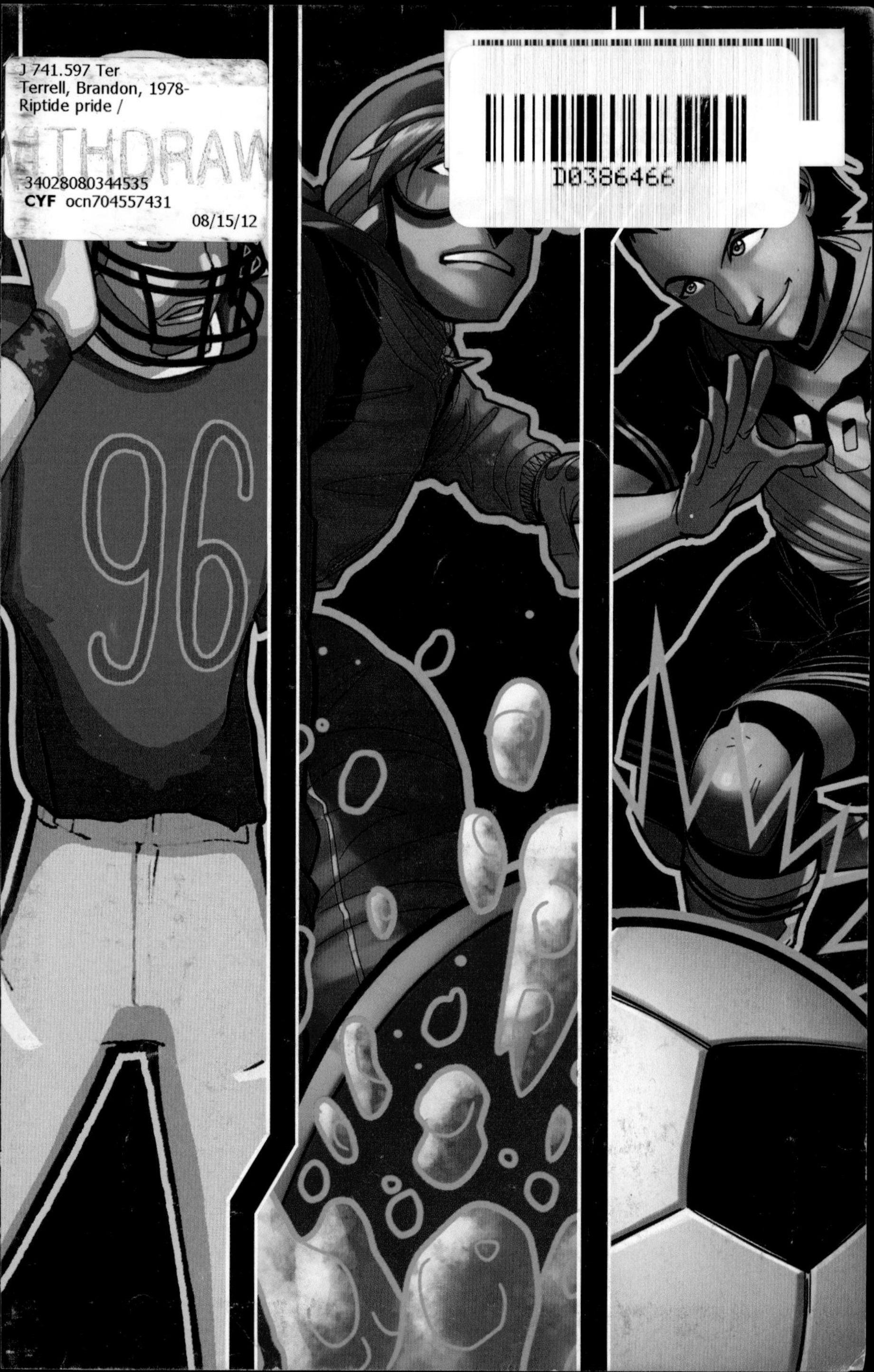
96

UP NEXT ›››

on Sports Illustrated KIDS

:02 SPORTS ZONE SPECIAL REPORT

:04 FEATURE PRESENTATION:

RIPTIDE PRIDE

FOLLOWED BY:

:50 SPORTS ZONE POSTGAME RECAP

:51 SPORTS ZONE POSTGAME EXTRA

:52 SI KIDS INFO CENTER

BREAKER BAY DECLARED OFF-LIMITS TO SURFERS DUE TO HIG SIK TICKER

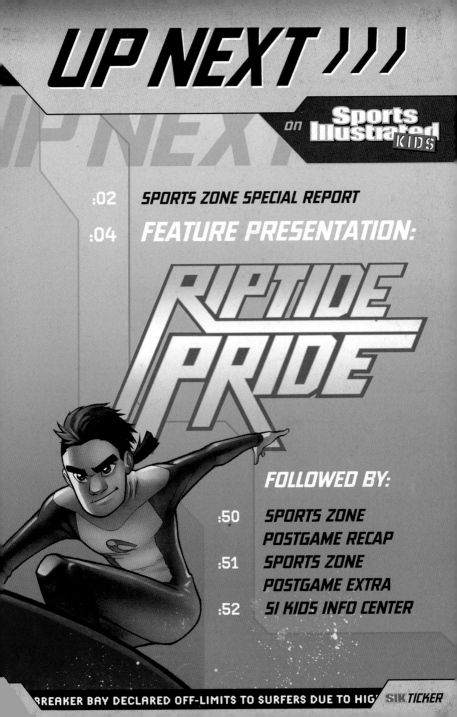

SPORTS ZONE

ECIAL REPORT

TEENS TO BRAVE BREAKER BAY'S DEADLY WAVES

TANE KALANA

STATS:
AGE: 14

BIO: Like many athletes, Tane is very superstitious. He believes his surfboard, Lucy, is the only reason he's any good at surfing. However, Tane is as laid back and relaxed as they get. He'd rather surf some waves and relax on the beach than pretty much anything else. But when Cody Hannigan challenges Tane to a surf-off on Breaker Bay, Tane balks. The jagged rocks and strong undertow are dangerous even on the luckiest day.

Sports Illustrated KIDS

UP NEXT: RIPTIDE PRIDE

CODY BRANNIGAN

AGE: 14

BIO: Everyone knows that Cody is a talented surfer, but no one's sure when he's telling the truth about his surfing stories. He has been known to exaggerate, and can also be a bit of a bully at times.

BLZ vs BRS
3·1
TGR vs ROR
33:32
EAG vs BAN
14·7
SPA vs WLD
4·3
BAN vs ROR
21·15
RZR vs LIG
4·3
BLZ vs BRS
3·1

LIA SAGE

AGE: 14

BIO: Tane's best friend and surfing buddy, Lia, is confident and relaxed on — and off — the waves.

OLIVER THOMAS

AGE: 14

BIO: Ollie is one of Cody's buddies. He tends to go with the flow and almost always agrees with anything Cody says.

LUCY

BRAND: CRESCENT FRESH SURFING, INC.

BIO: Lucy is Tane's lucky surfboard. Originally, the board belonged to Summer Kalana, Tane's mother, a former surfing champ.

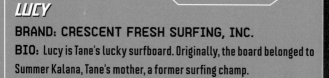

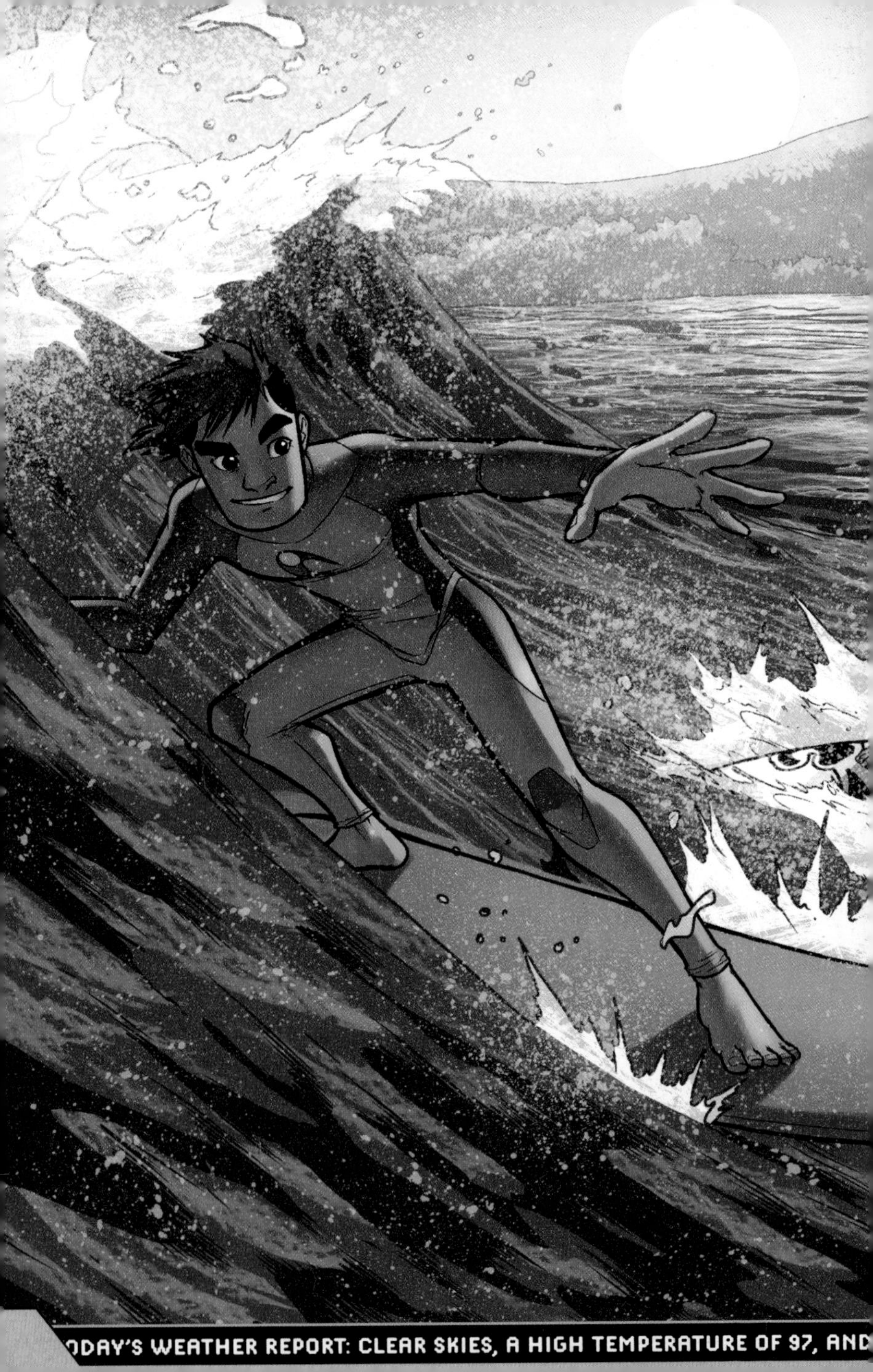
ODAY'S WEATHER REPORT: CLEAR SKIES, A HIGH TEMPERATURE OF 97, AND

PRESENTS

A PRODUCTION OF

STONE ARCH BOOKS
a capstone imprint

written by Brandon Terrell
penciled by Fernando Cano
inked by Andres Esparza
colored by Fernando Cano

designed and directed by Bob Lentz
edited by Sean Tulien
creative direction by Heather Kindseth
editorial management by Donald Lemke
editorial direction by Michael Dahl

Sports Illustrated KIDS *Riptide Pride* is published by Stone Arch Books,
151 Good Counsel Drive, P.O. Box 669, Mankato, Minnesota 56002.
www.capstonepub.com

Copyright © 2012 by Stone Arch Books, a Capstone imprint.

All rights reserved. No part of this publication may be reproduced in whole or in
part, or stored in a retrieval system, or transmitted in any form or by any means,
electronic, mechanical, photocopying, recording, or otherwise, without written
permission of the publisher, or where applicable Time Inc.
For information regarding permissions, write to Stone Arch Books,
151 Good Counsel Drive, P.O. Box 669, Dept. R, Mankato, Minnesota 56002.
SI KIDS is a trademark of Time Inc. Used with permission.

Printed in the United States of America in Stevens Point, Wisconsin.
032011   006111WZF11

Summary: Tane Kalana rides waves with ease and looks good doing it.
But being talented tends to put a target on your back, and Cody Hannigan
has his sights set on taking Tane down a notch. Cody challenges him to a
surfer showdown — at Breaker Bay! The infamous surfing locale is known
to be unpredictable and dangerous, but Tane is tired of Cody's bullying.

Library of Congress Cataloging-in-Publication Data
Terrell, Brandon, 1978-
  Riptide pride / written by Brandon Terrell ; illustrated by Fernando Cano,
Andres Esparza
    p. cm. -- (Sports illustrated kids graphic novels)
    ISBN 978-1-4342-2238-1 (library binding) -- ISBN 978-1-4342-3399-8 (pbk.)
  1. Surfing--Comic books, strips, etc. 2. Surfing--Juvenile fiction. 3. Pride
and vanity--Comic books, strips, etc. [1. Graphic novels. 2. Surfing--Fiction.
3. Pride and vanity--Fiction. 4. Hawaii--Fiction.] I. Cano, Fernando, ill. II.
Esparza, Andres, ill. IV. Title. V. Series: Sports illustrated kids graphic
novels.
    PZ7.7.T46Ri 2012
    741.5'973--dc22   2011008308

YES! IT'S GOING TO BE A PERFECT DAY FOR SURFING, SO GRAB YOUR

SIK TICKER

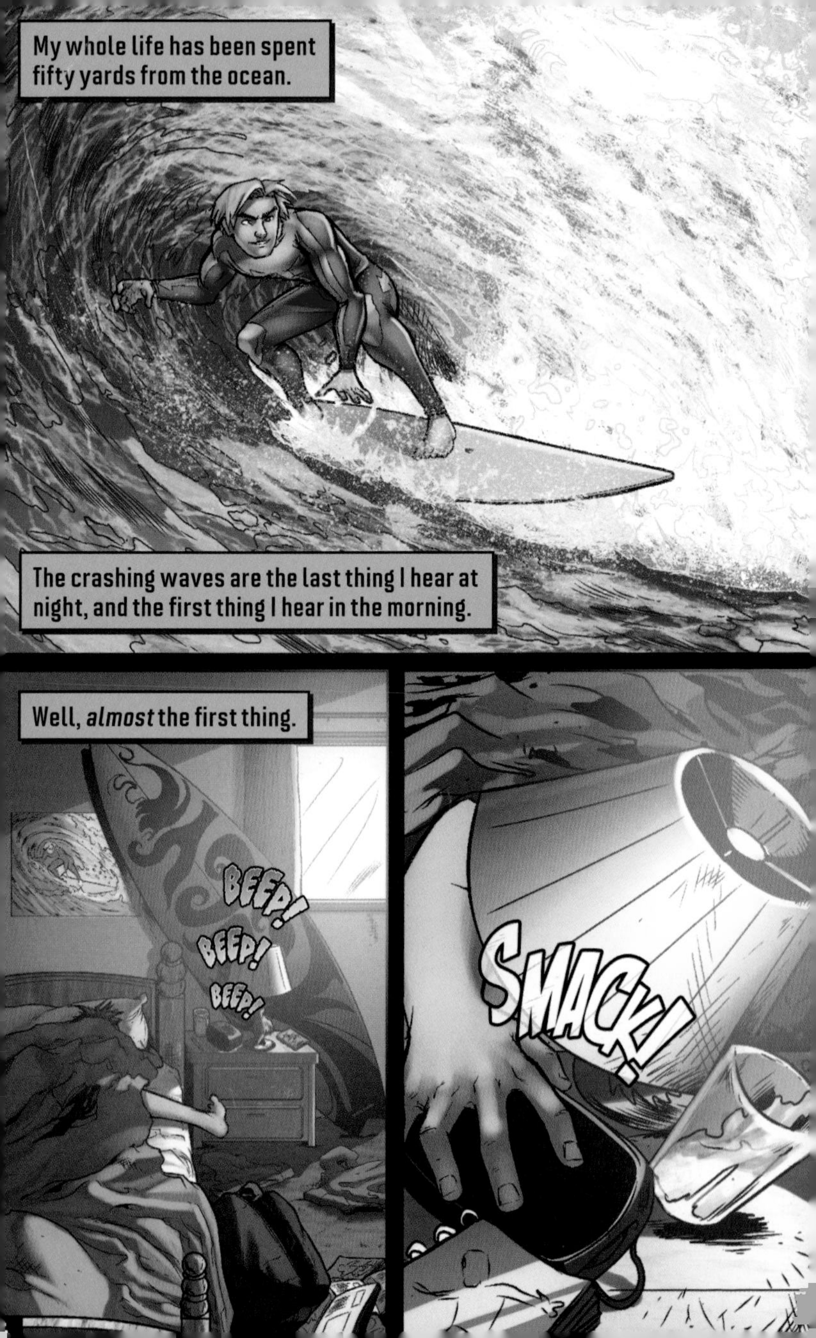
My whole life has been spent fifty yards from the ocean.
The crashing waves are the last thing I hear at night, and the first thing I hear in the morning.
Well, *almost* the first thing.
BEEP!
BEEP!
BEEP!
SMACK!

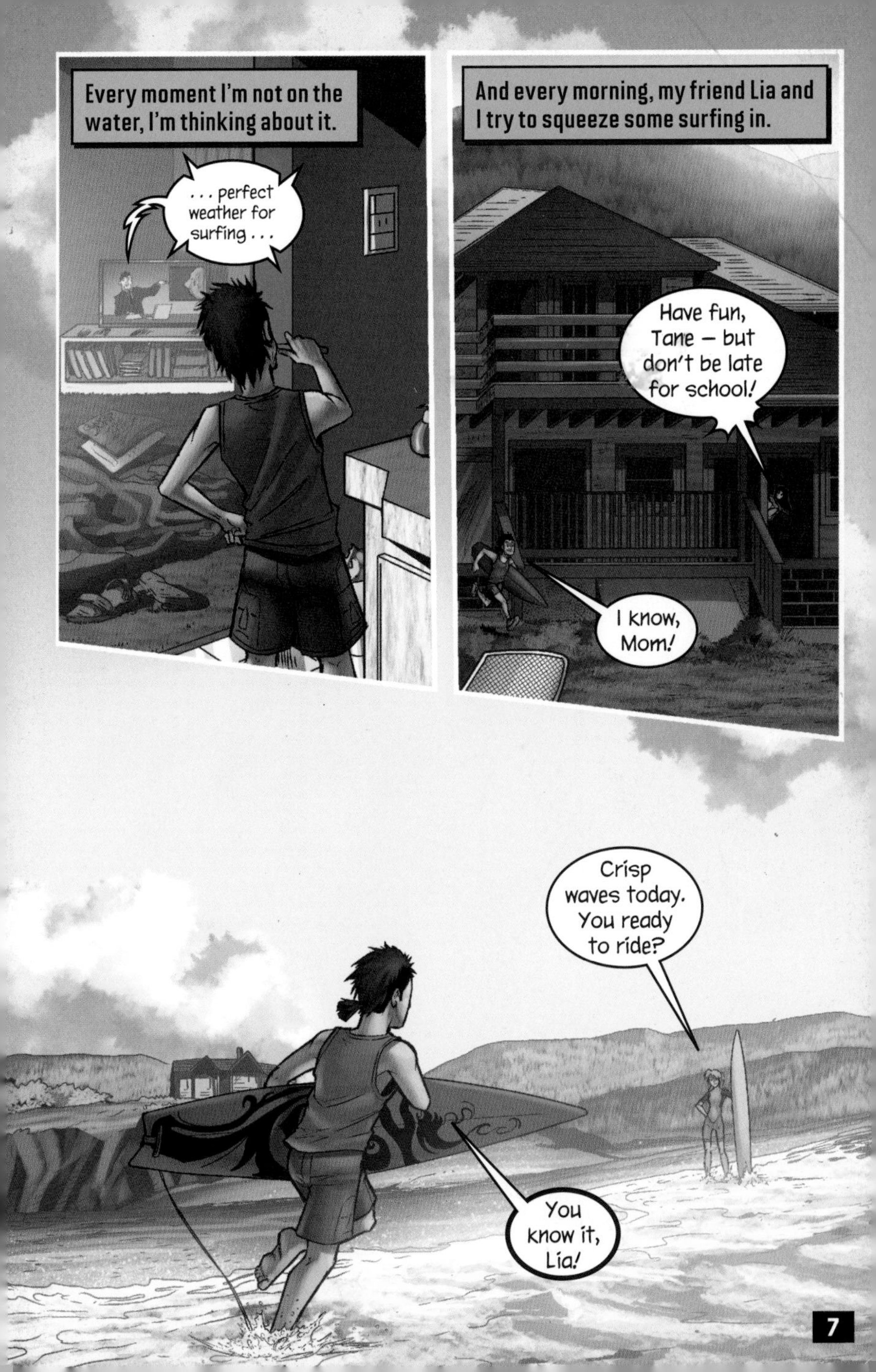

Every moment I'm not on the water, I'm thinking about it.
. . . perfect weather for surfing . . .
And every morning, my friend Lia and I try to squeeze some surfing in.
Have fun, Tane — but don't be late for school!
I know, Mom!
Crisp waves today. You ready to ride?
You know it, Lia!

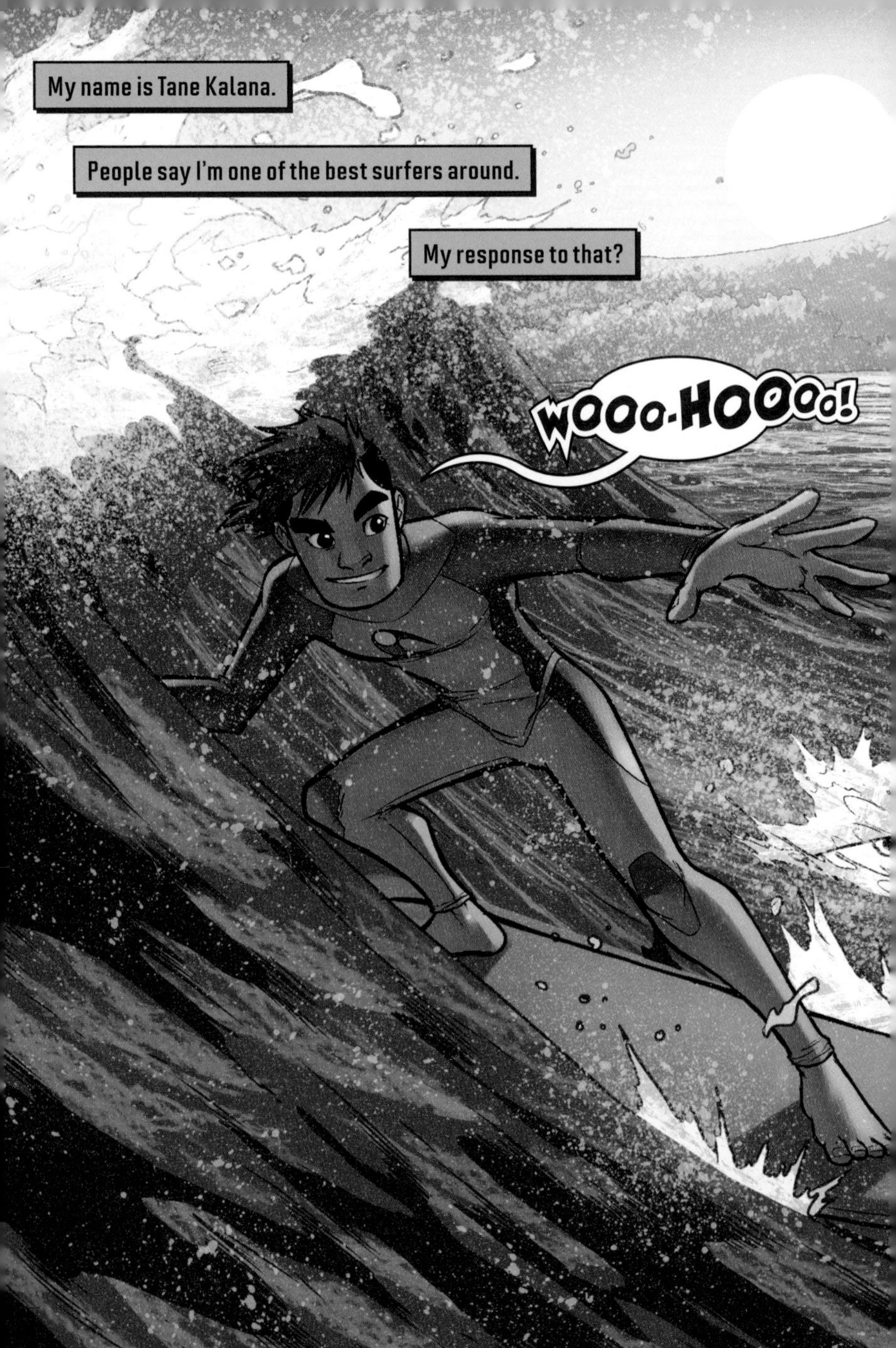
My name is Tane Kalana.
People say I'm one of the best surfers around.
My response to that?
WOOO-HOOOOO!

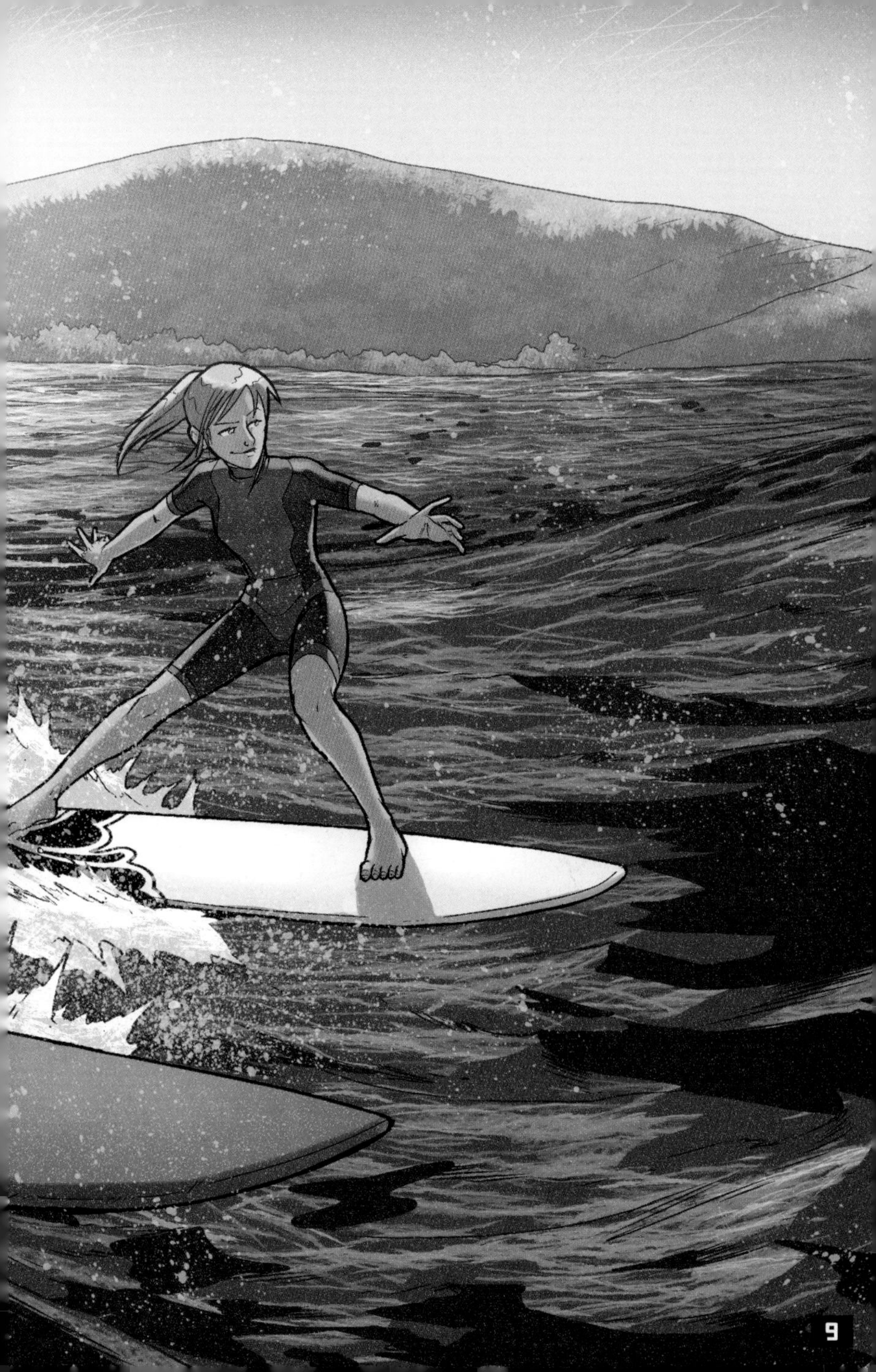

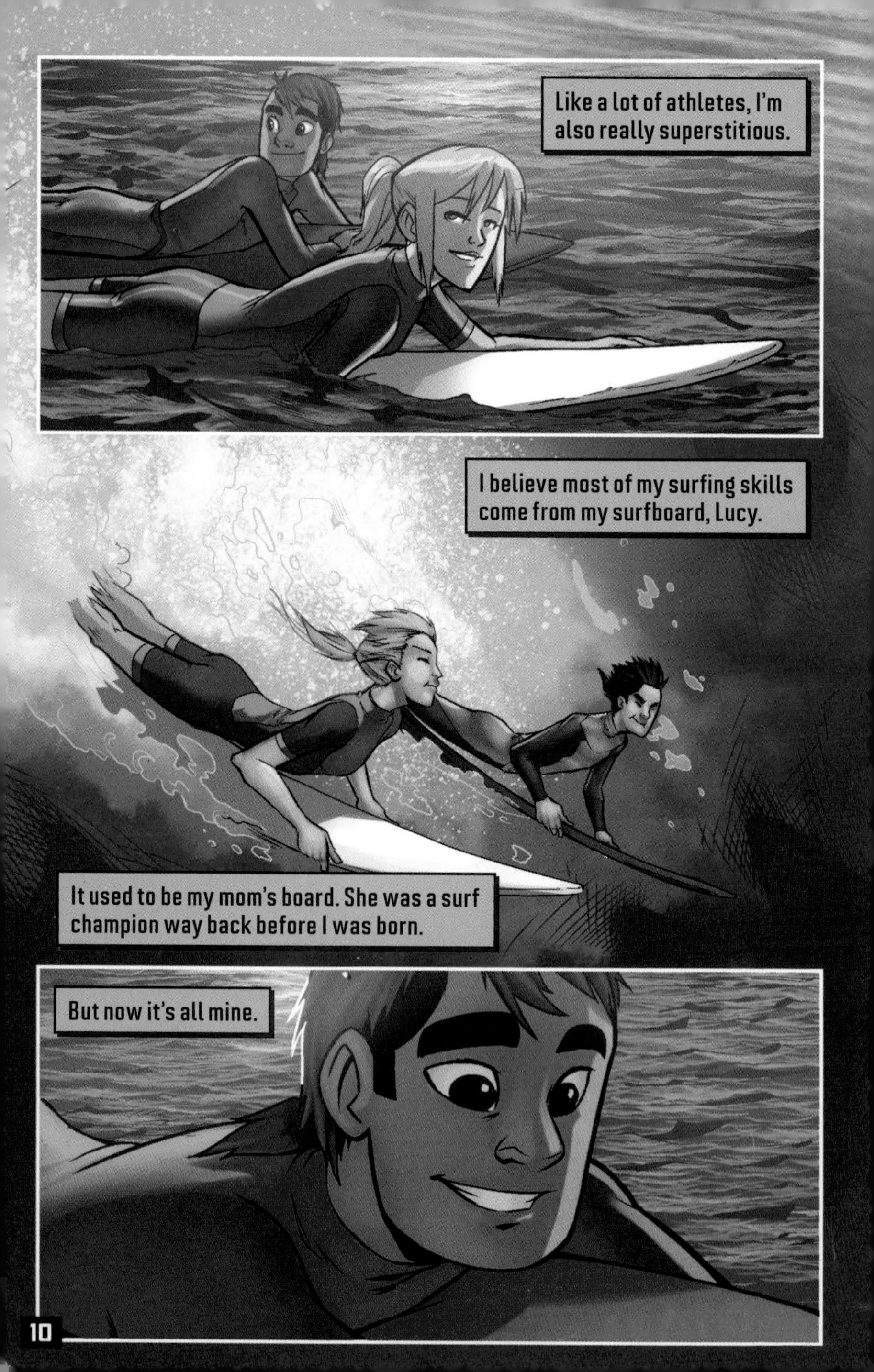
Like a lot of athletes, I'm also really superstitious.
I believe most of my surfing skills come from my surfboard, Lucy.
It used to be my mom's board. She was a surf champion way back before I was born.
But now it's all mine.

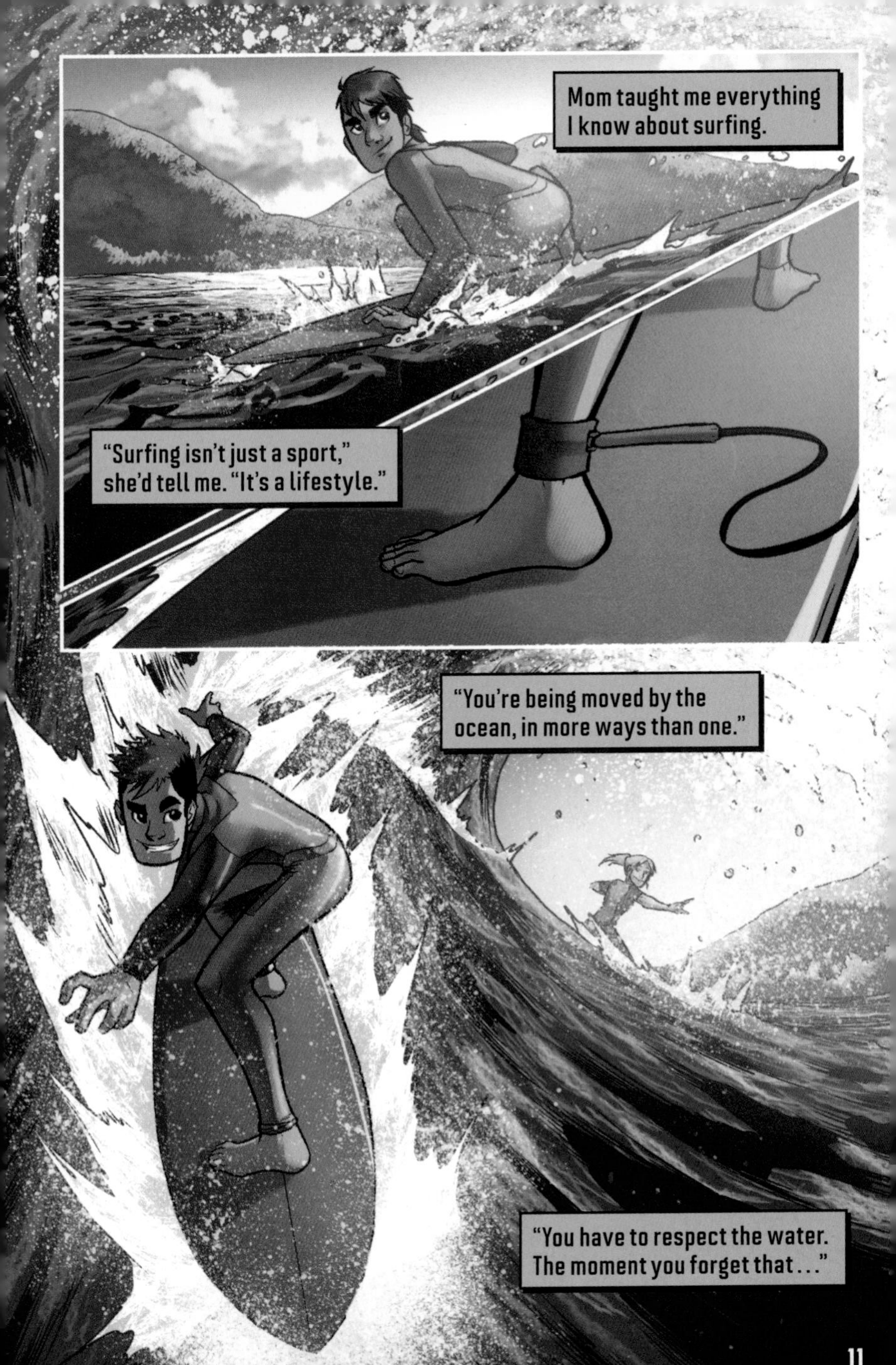
Mom taught me everything I know about surfing.
"Surfing isn't just a sport," she'd tell me. "It's a lifestyle."
"You're being moved by the ocean, in more ways than one."
"You have to respect the water. The moment you forget that . . ."

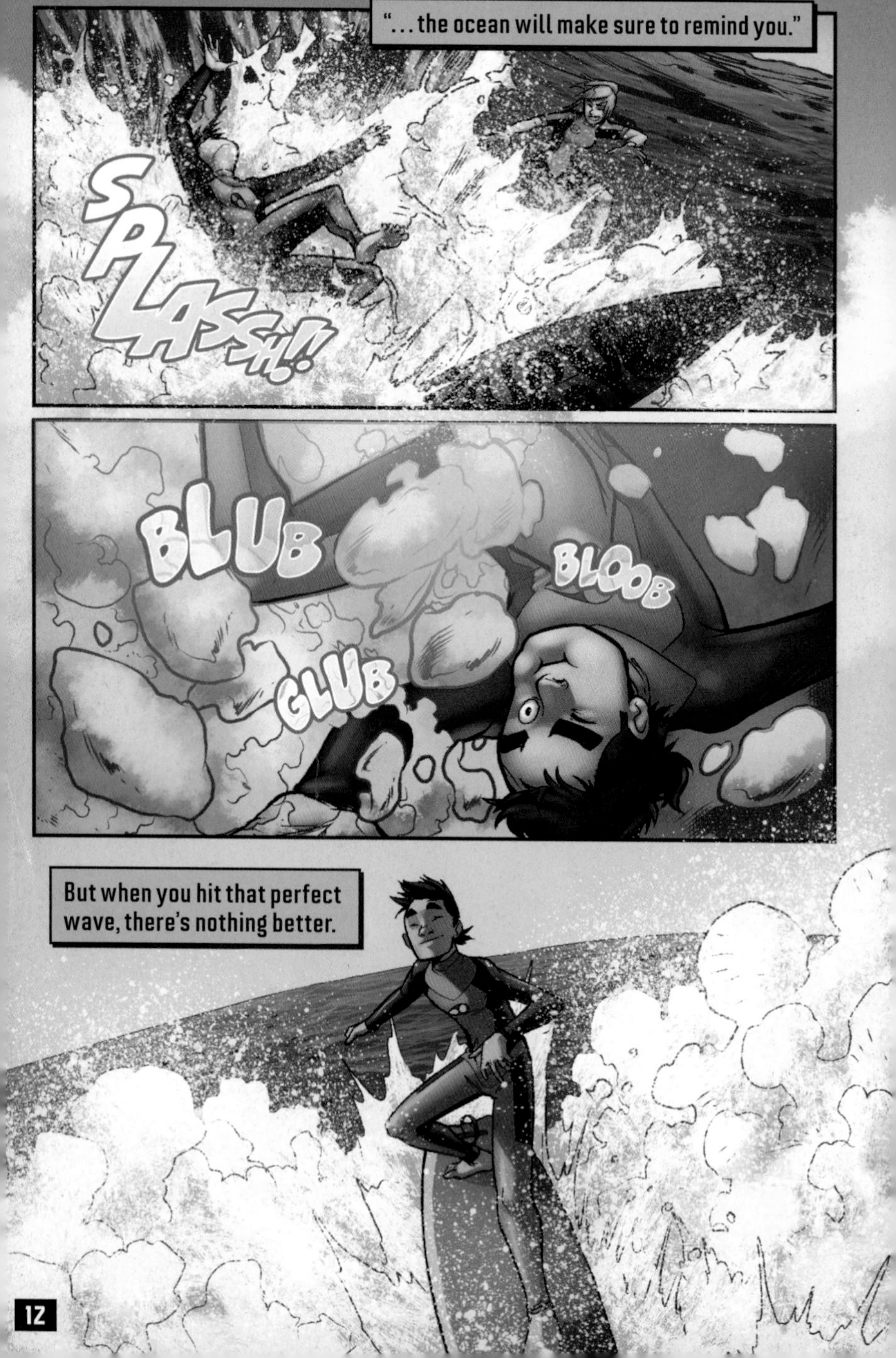
"...the ocean will make sure to remind you."
SPLASSH!!
BLUB
BLOOB
GLUB
But when you hit that perfect wave, there's nothing better.

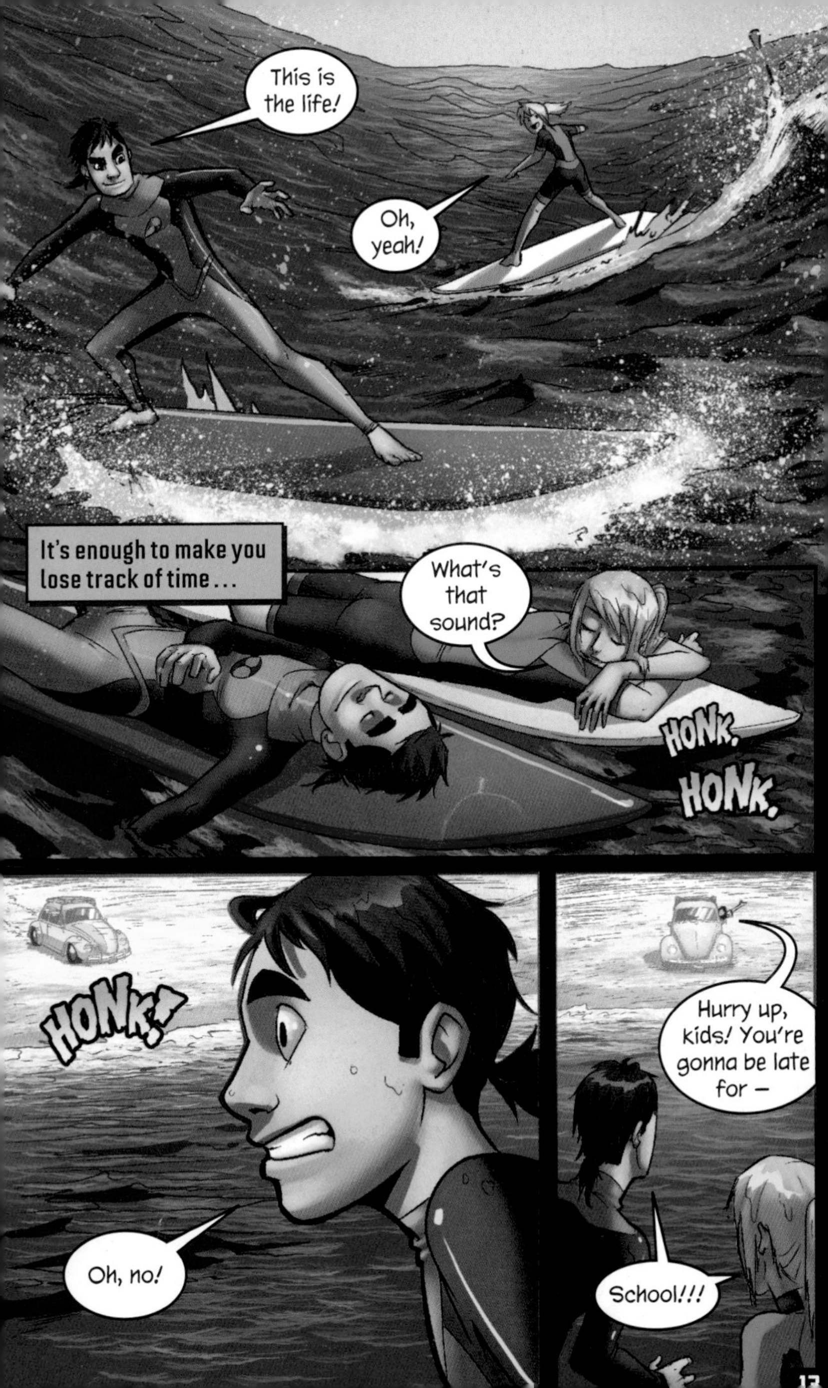
This is the life!
Oh, yeah!
It's enough to make you lose track of time . . .
What's that sound?
HONK. HONK.
HONK!
Oh, no!
Hurry up, kids! You're gonna be late for –
School!!!

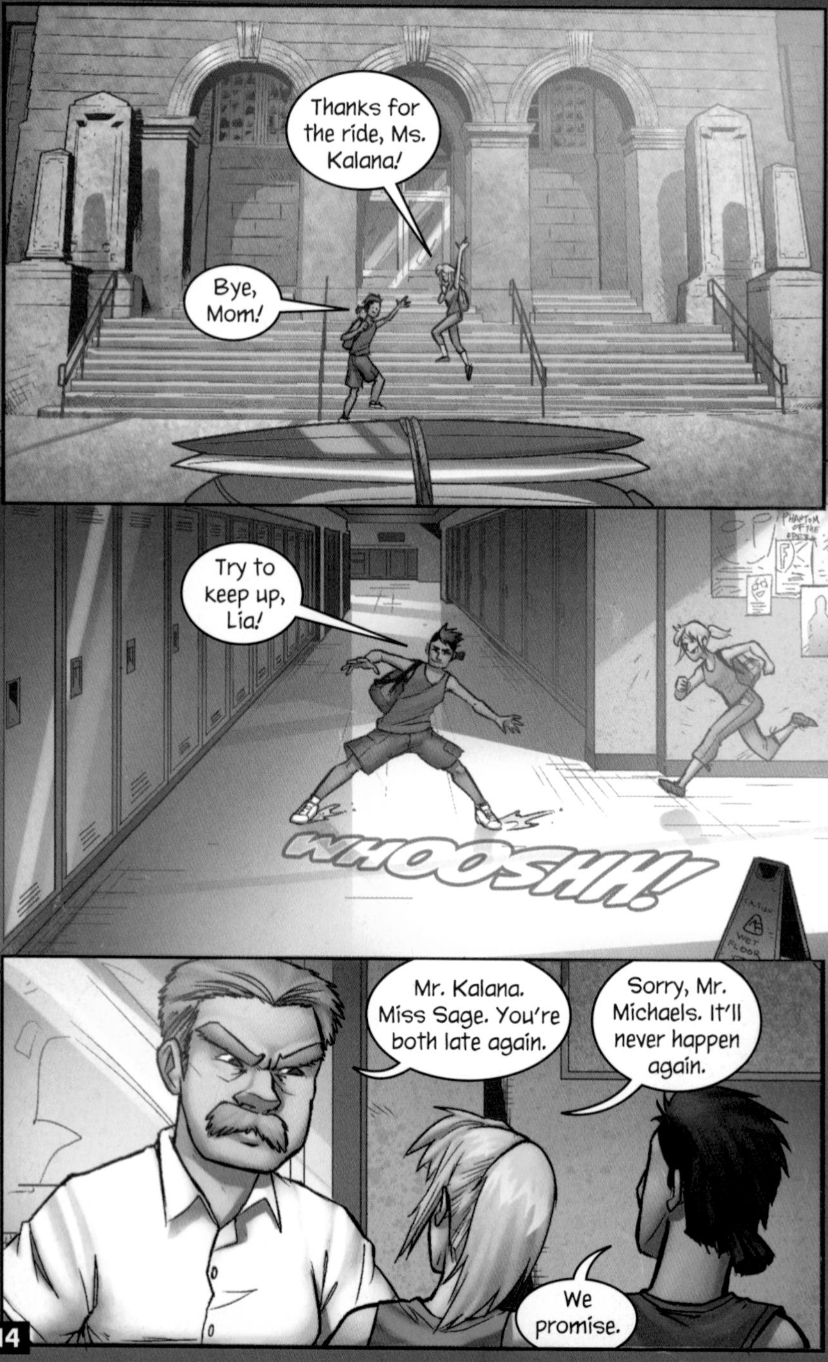
Thanks for the ride, Ms. Kalana!
Bye, Mom!
Try to keep up, Lia!
WHOOSHH!
Mr. Kalana. Miss Sage. You're both late again.
Sorry, Mr. Michaels. It'll never happen again.
We promise.

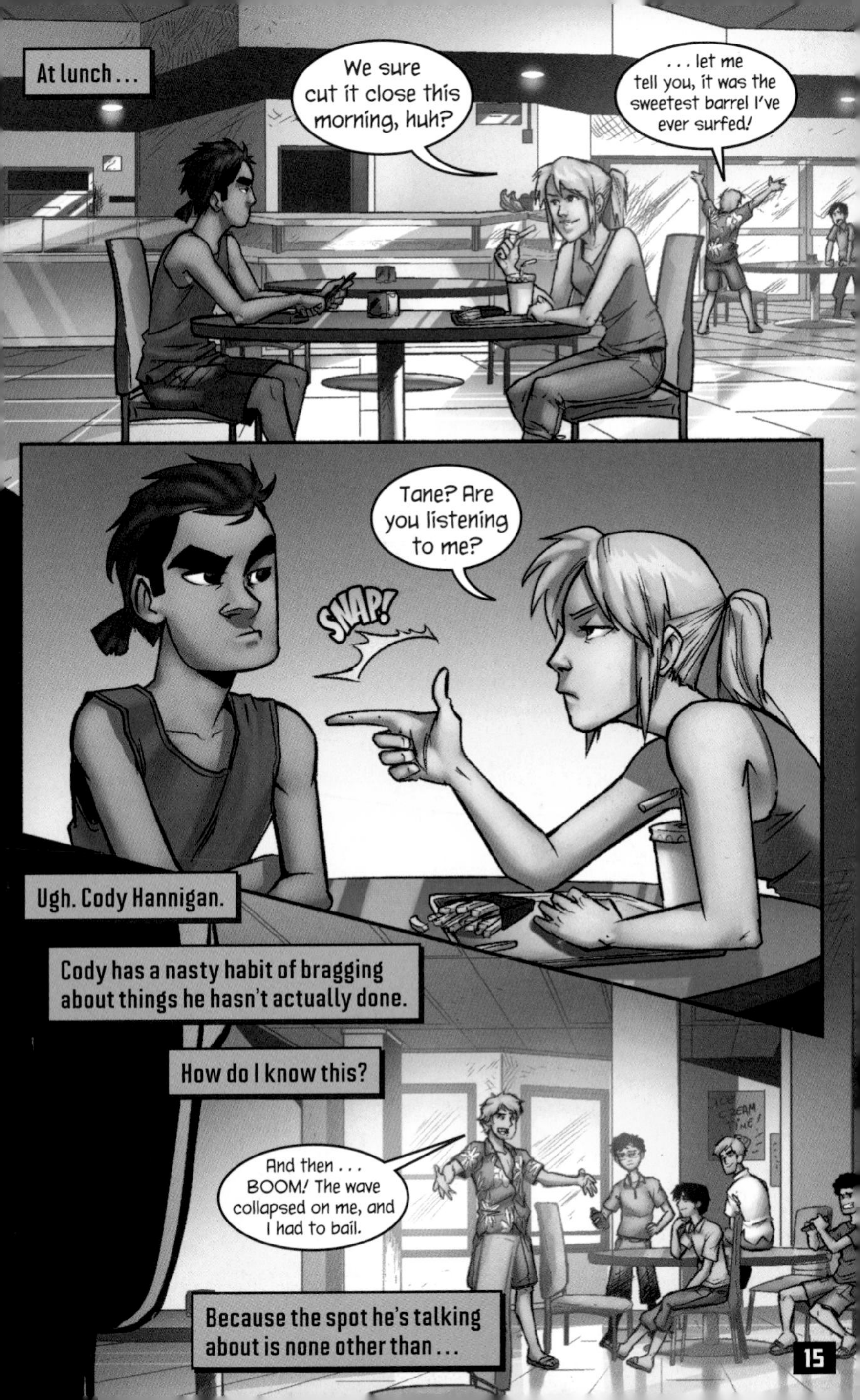

At lunch . . .
We sure cut it close this morning, huh?
. . . let me tell you, it was the sweetest barrel I've ever surfed!
Tane? Are you listening to me?
SNAP!
Ugh. Cody Hannigan.
Cody has a nasty habit of bragging about things he hasn't actually done.
How do I know this?
And then . . . BOOM! The wave collapsed on me, and I had to bail.
Because the spot he's talking about is none other than . . .

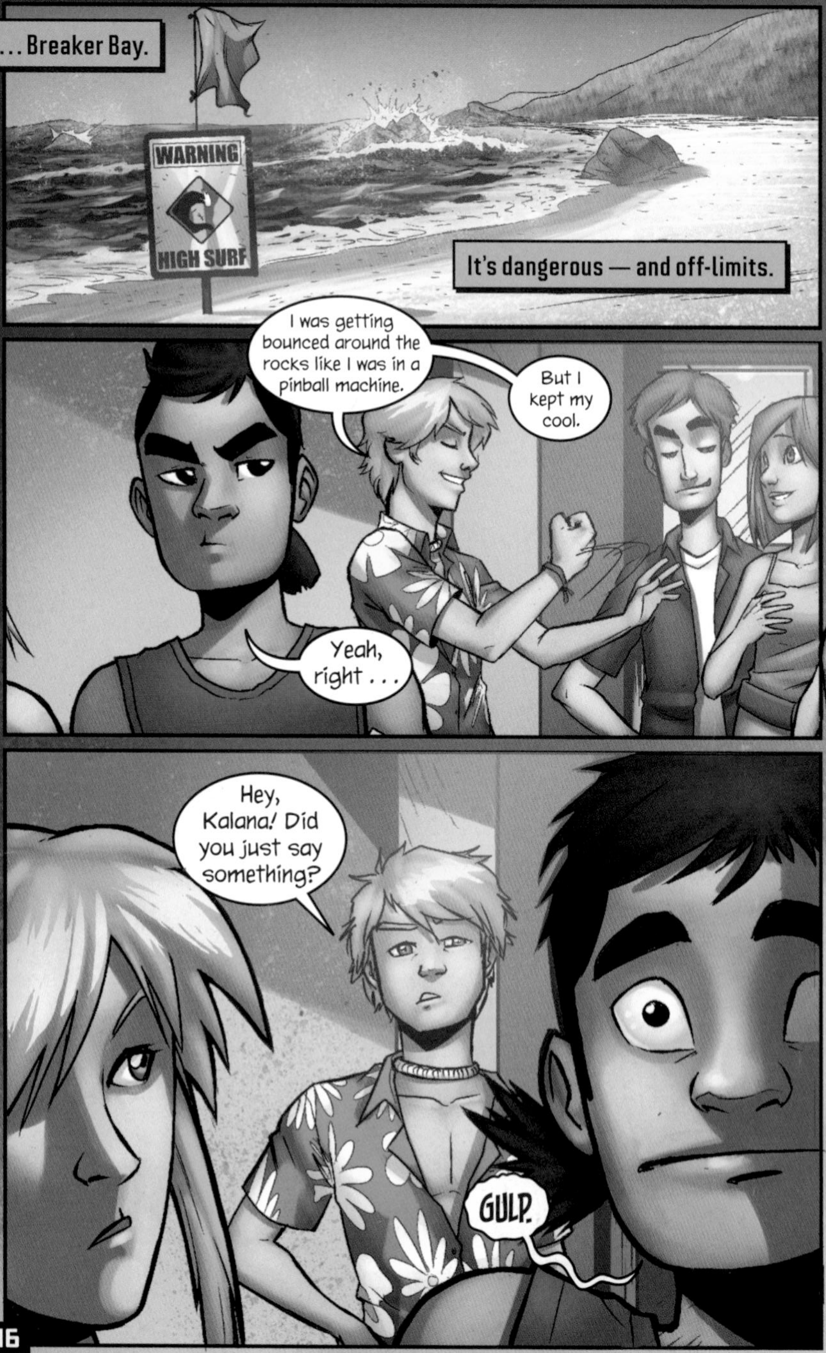
. . . Breaker Bay.
WARNING
HIGH SURF
It's dangerous — and off-limits.
I was getting bounced around the rocks like I was in a pinball machine.
But I kept my cool.
Yeah, right . . .
Hey, Kalana! Did you just say something?
GULP.

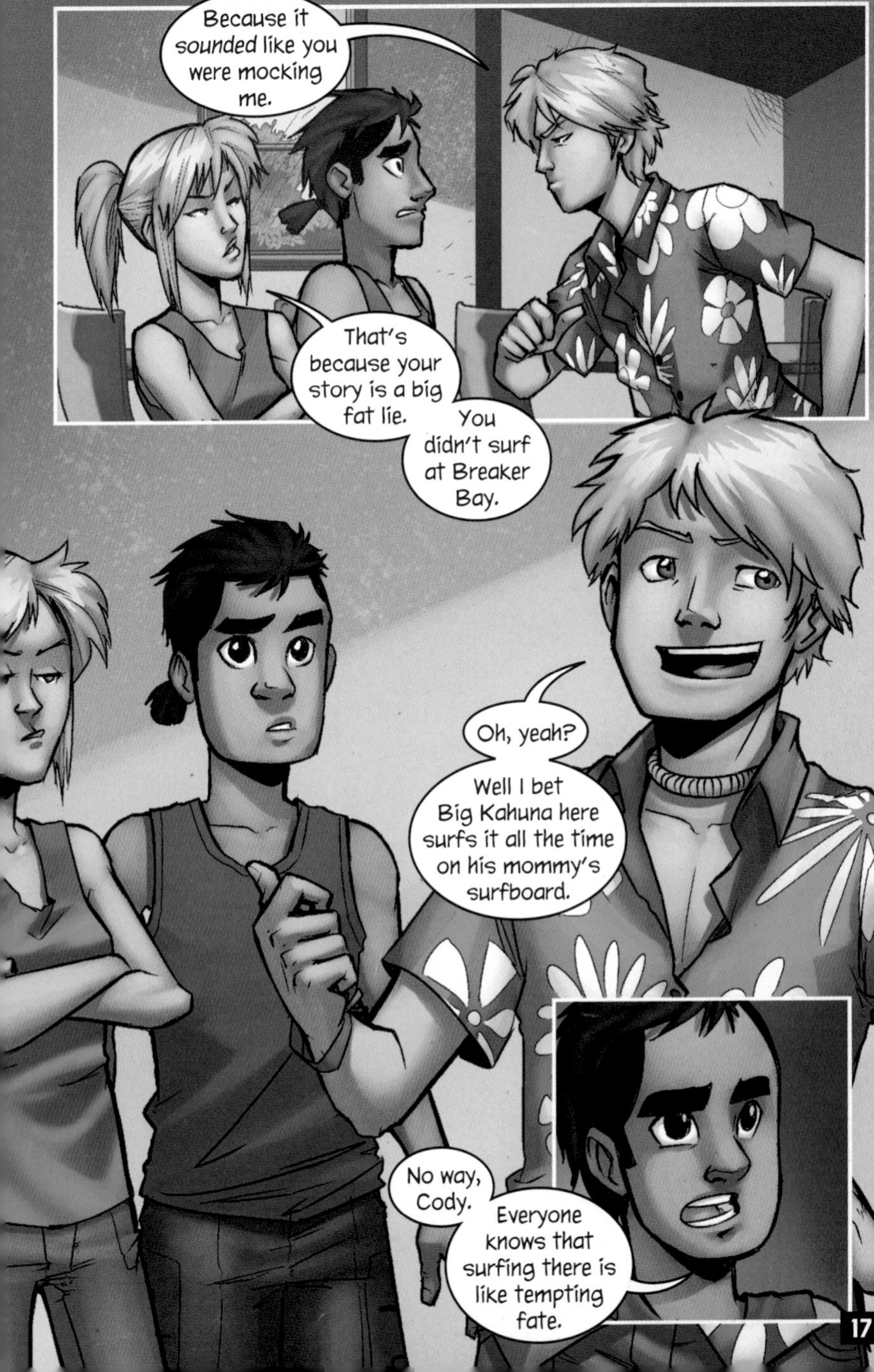
Because it sounded like you were mocking me.
That's because your story is a big fat lie.
You didn't surf at Breaker Bay.
Oh, yeah?
Well I bet Big Kahuna here surfs it all the time on his mommy's surfboard.
No way, Cody.
Everyone knows that surfing there is like tempting fate.

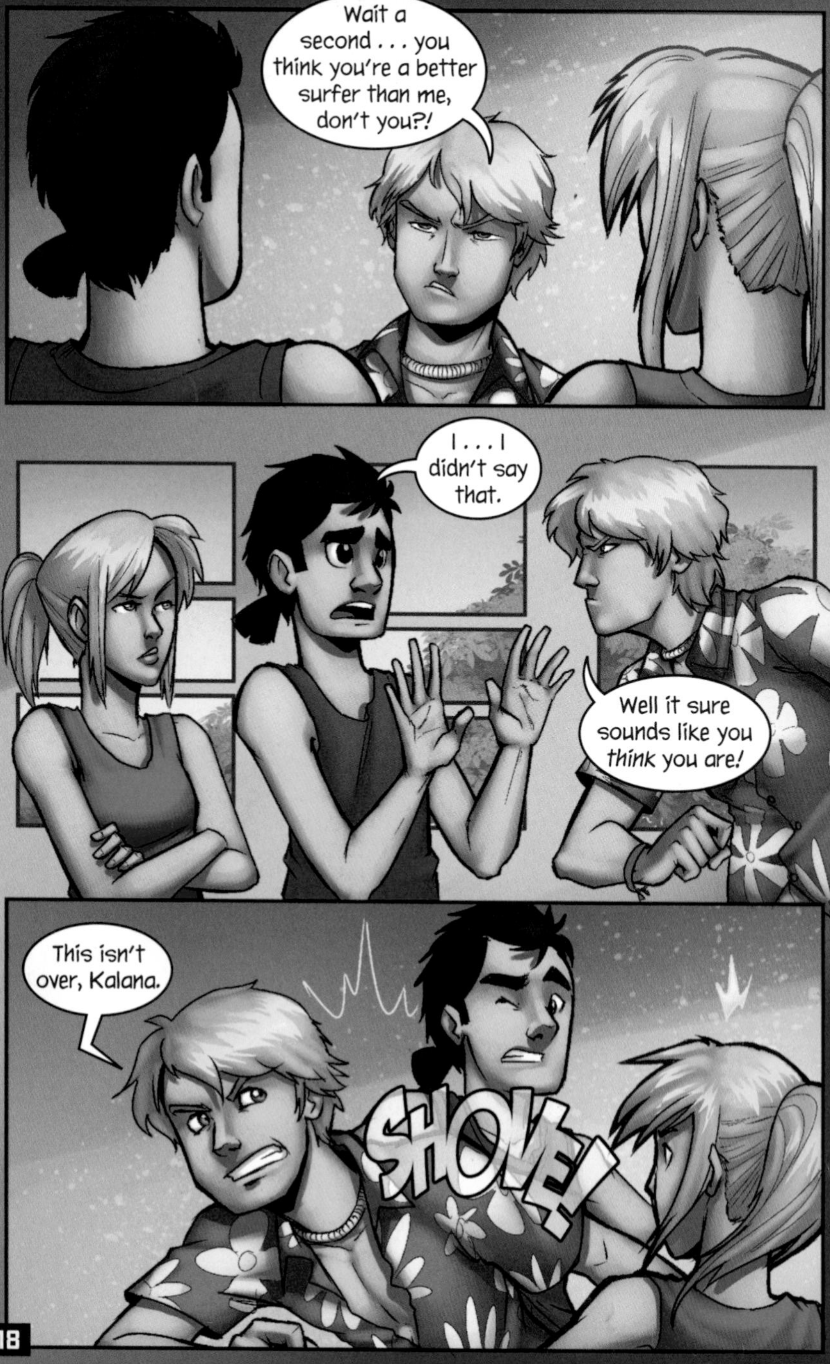
Wait a second . . . you think you're a better surfer than me, don't you?!
I . . . I didn't say that.
Well it sure sounds like you think you are!
This isn't over, Kalana.
SHOVE!

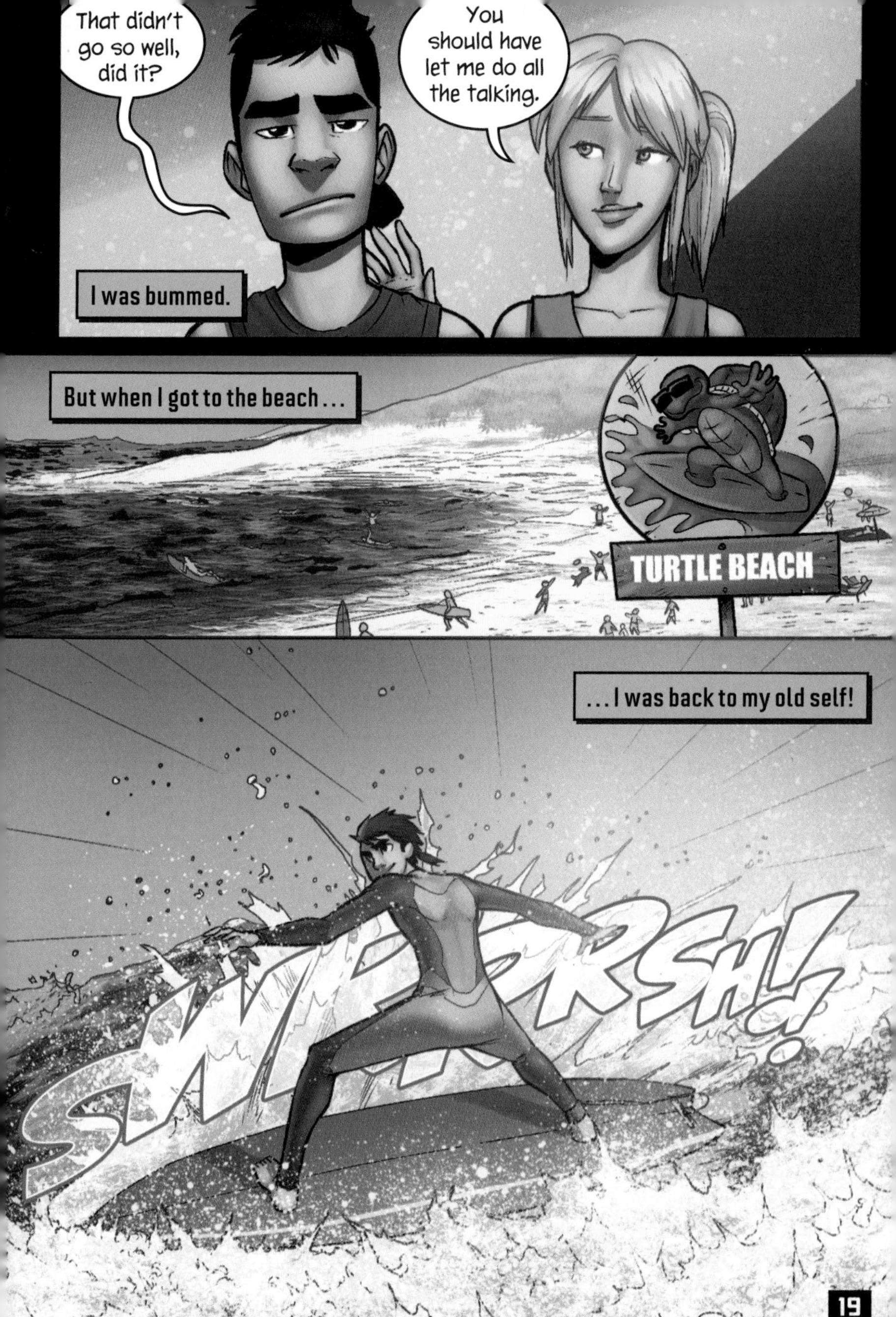
That didn't go so well, did it?
You should have let me do all the talking.
I was bummed.
But when I got to the beach . . .
TURTLE BEACH
. . . I was back to my old self!

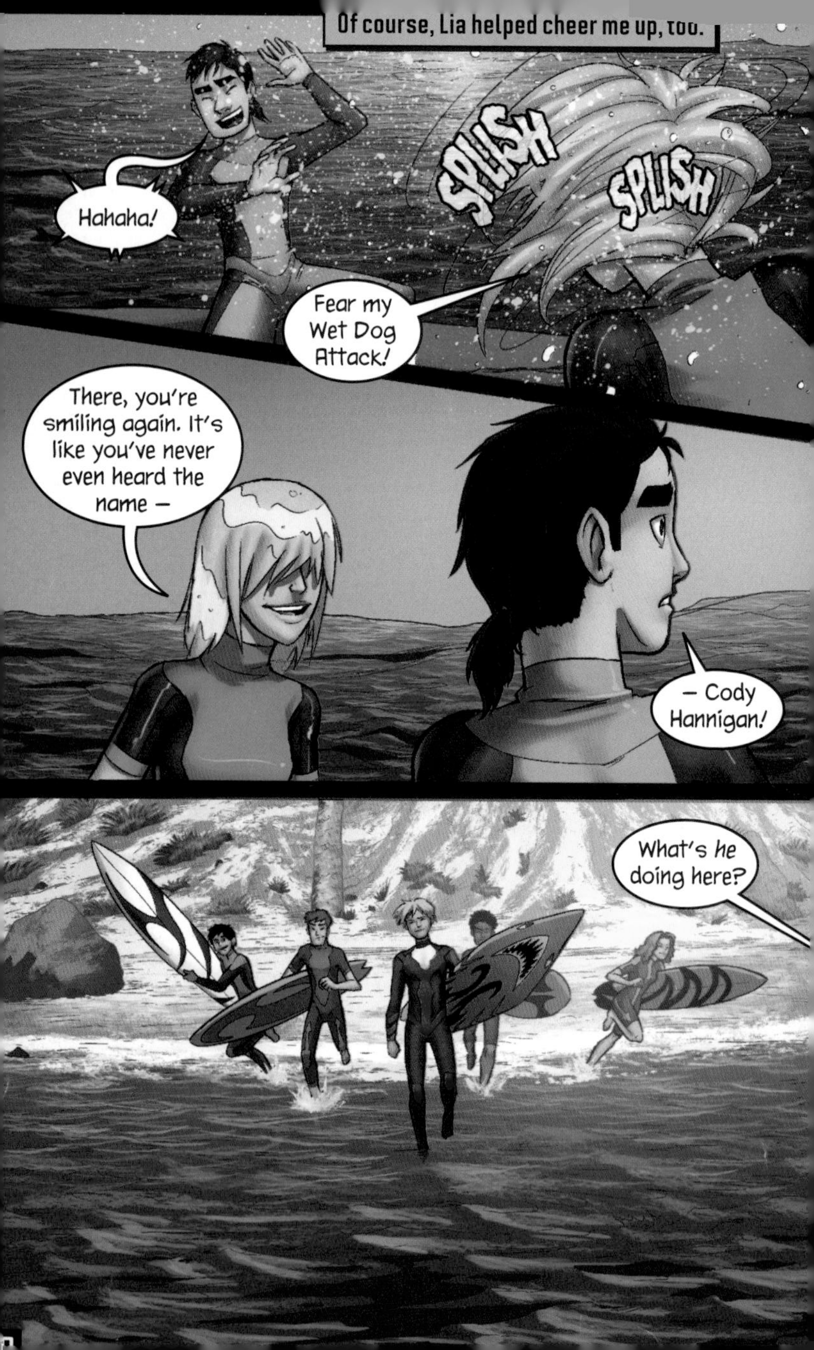

Of course, Lia helped cheer me up, too.
Hahaha!
SPLISH
SPLISH
Fear my Wet Dog Attack!
There, you're smiling again. It's like you've never even heard the name –
– Cody Hannigan!
What's he doing here?

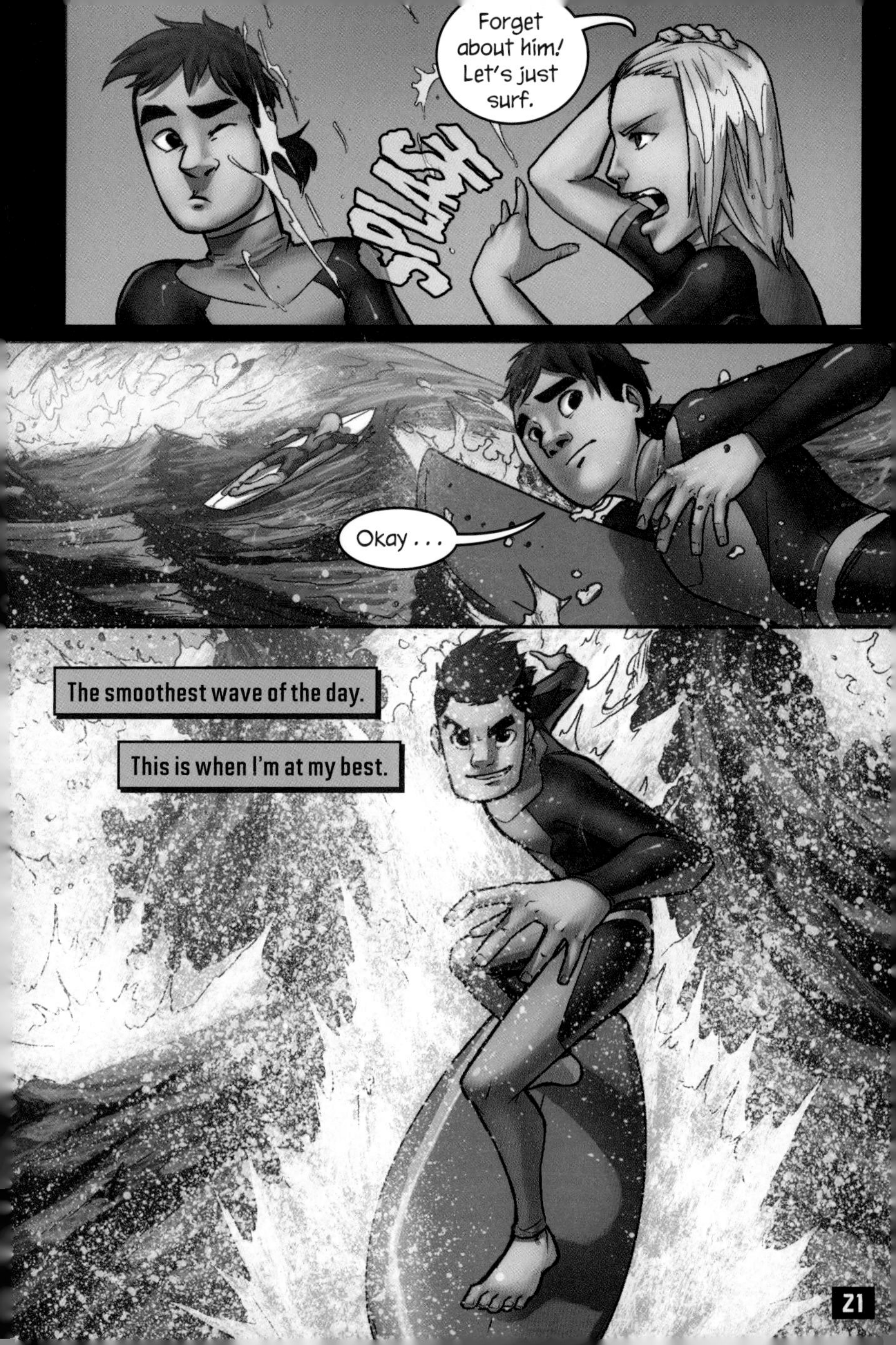

Forget about him! Let's just surf.
SPLASH
Okay . . .
The smoothest wave of the day.
This is when I'm at my best.

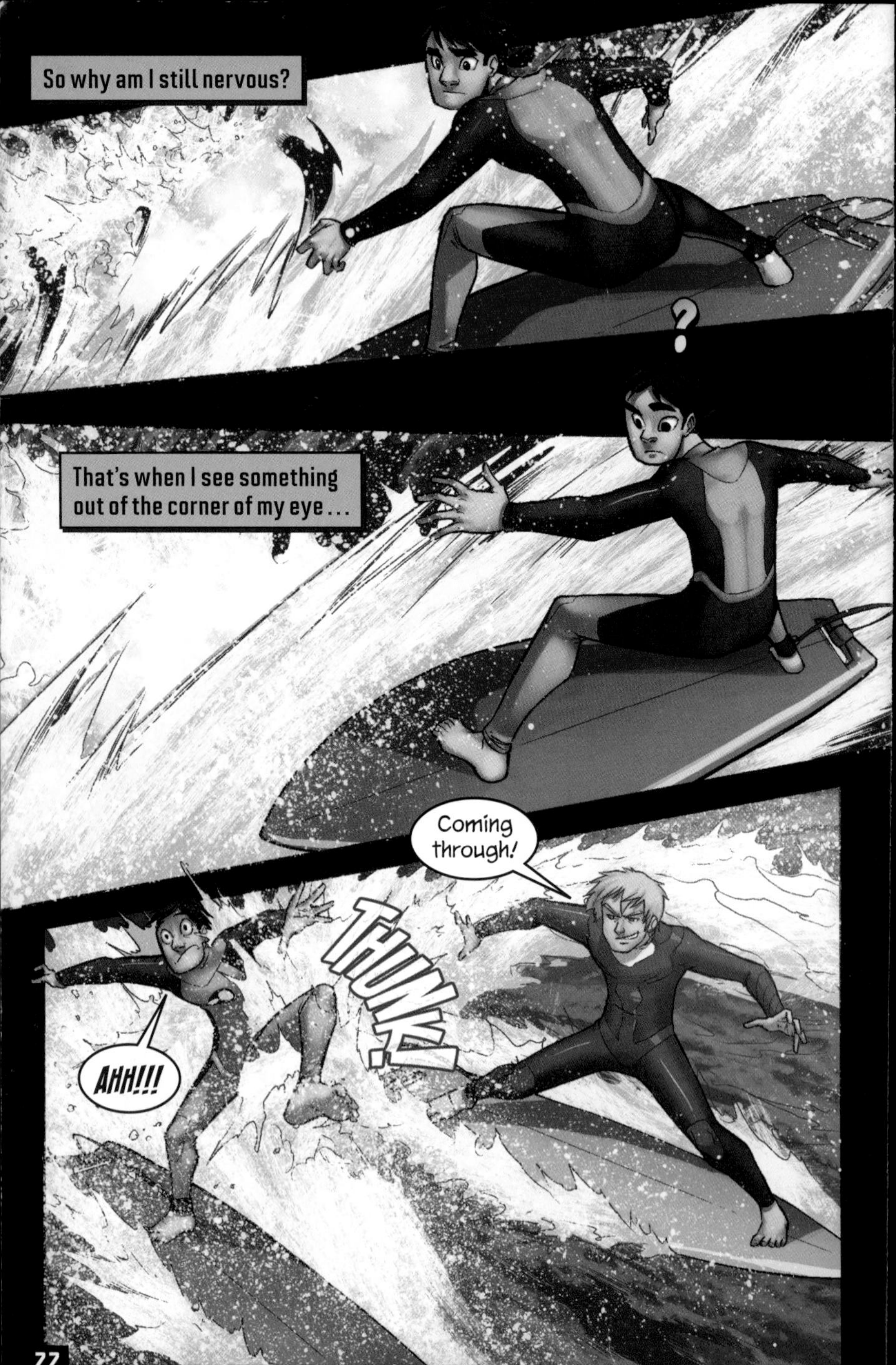
So why am I still nervous?
?
That's when I see something out of the corner of my eye . . .
Coming through!
THUNK!
AHH!!!

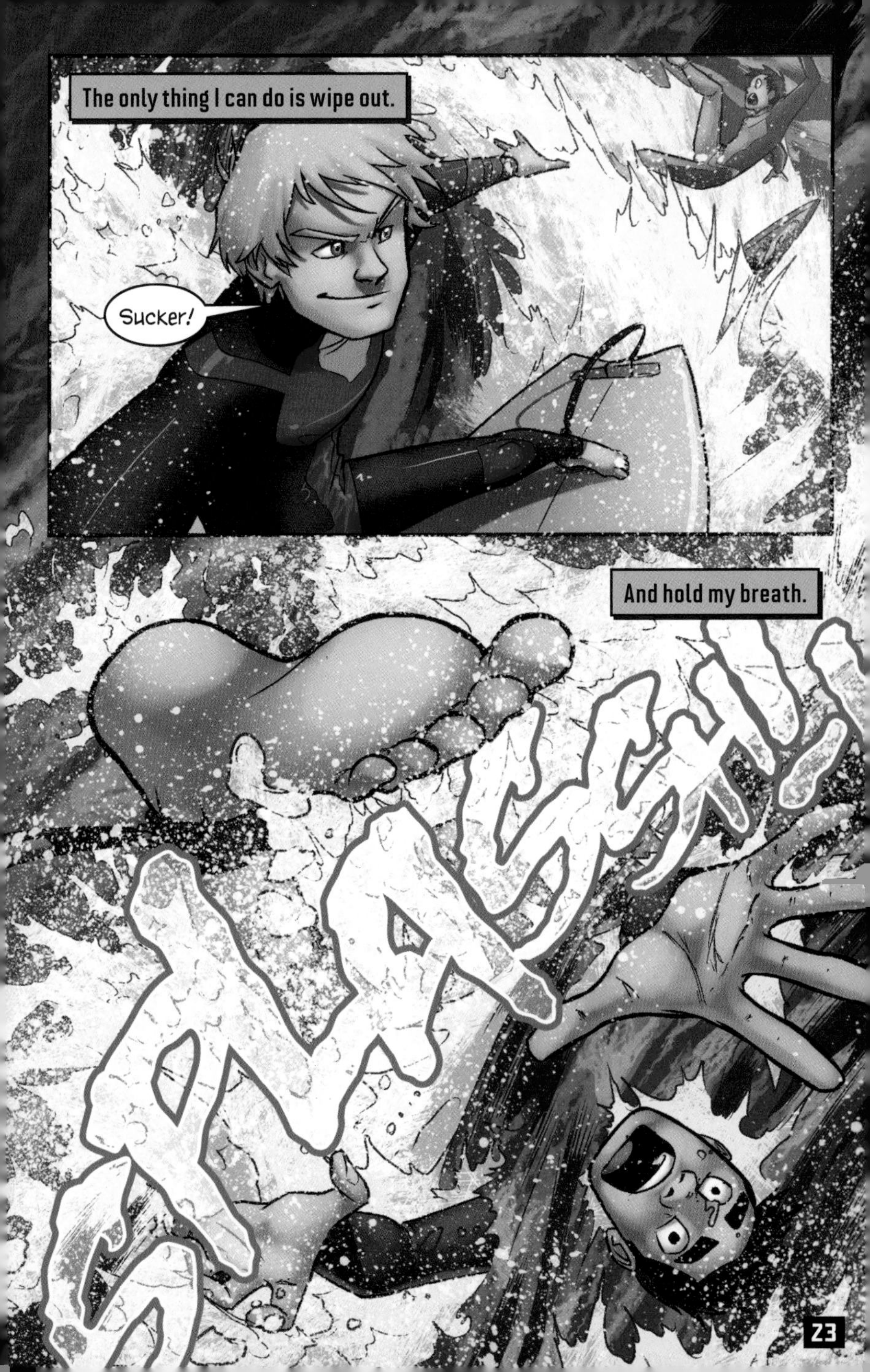
The only thing I can do is wipe out.
Sucker!
And hold my breath.

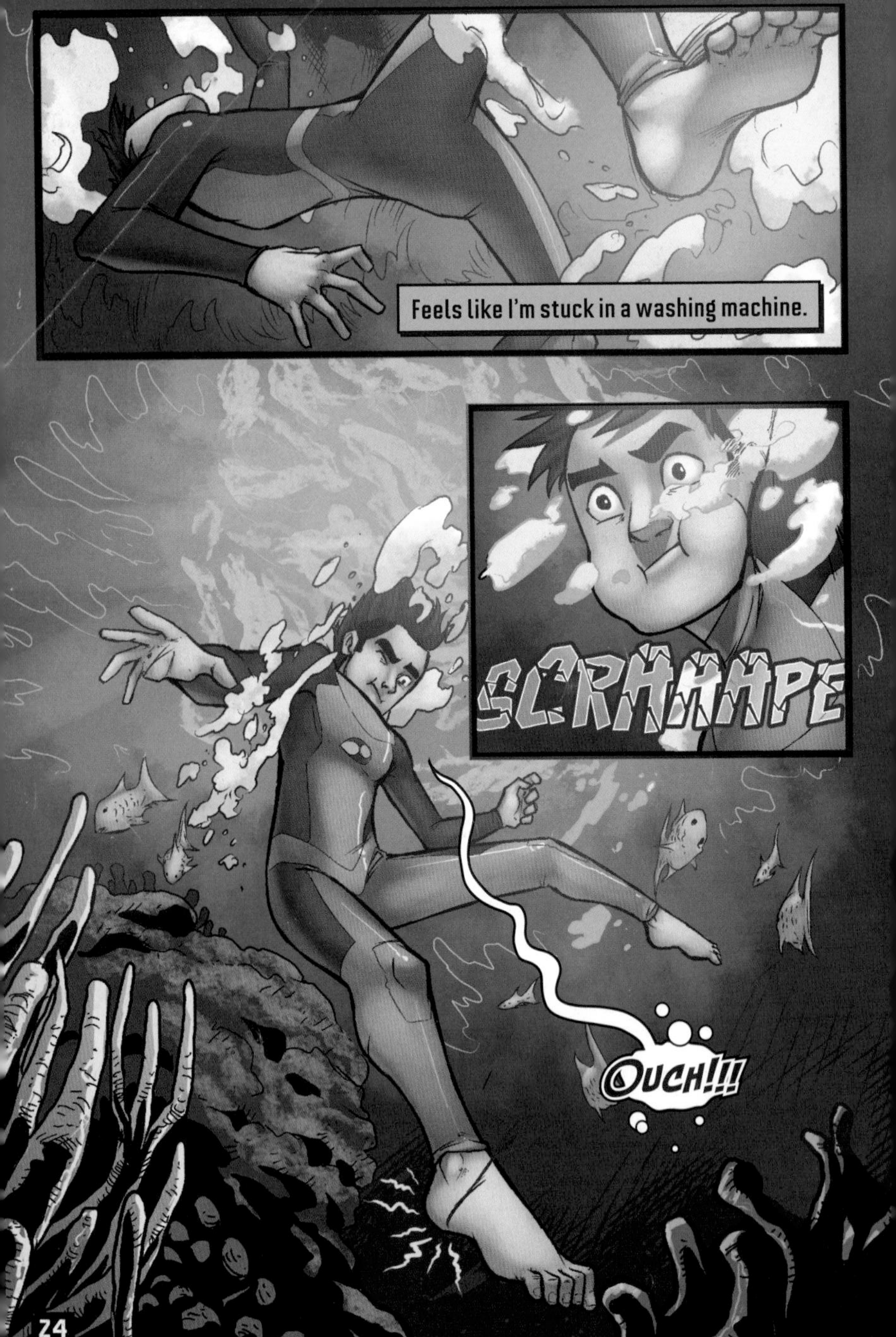

Feels like I'm stuck in a washing machine.
SCRAAAPE
OUCH!!!

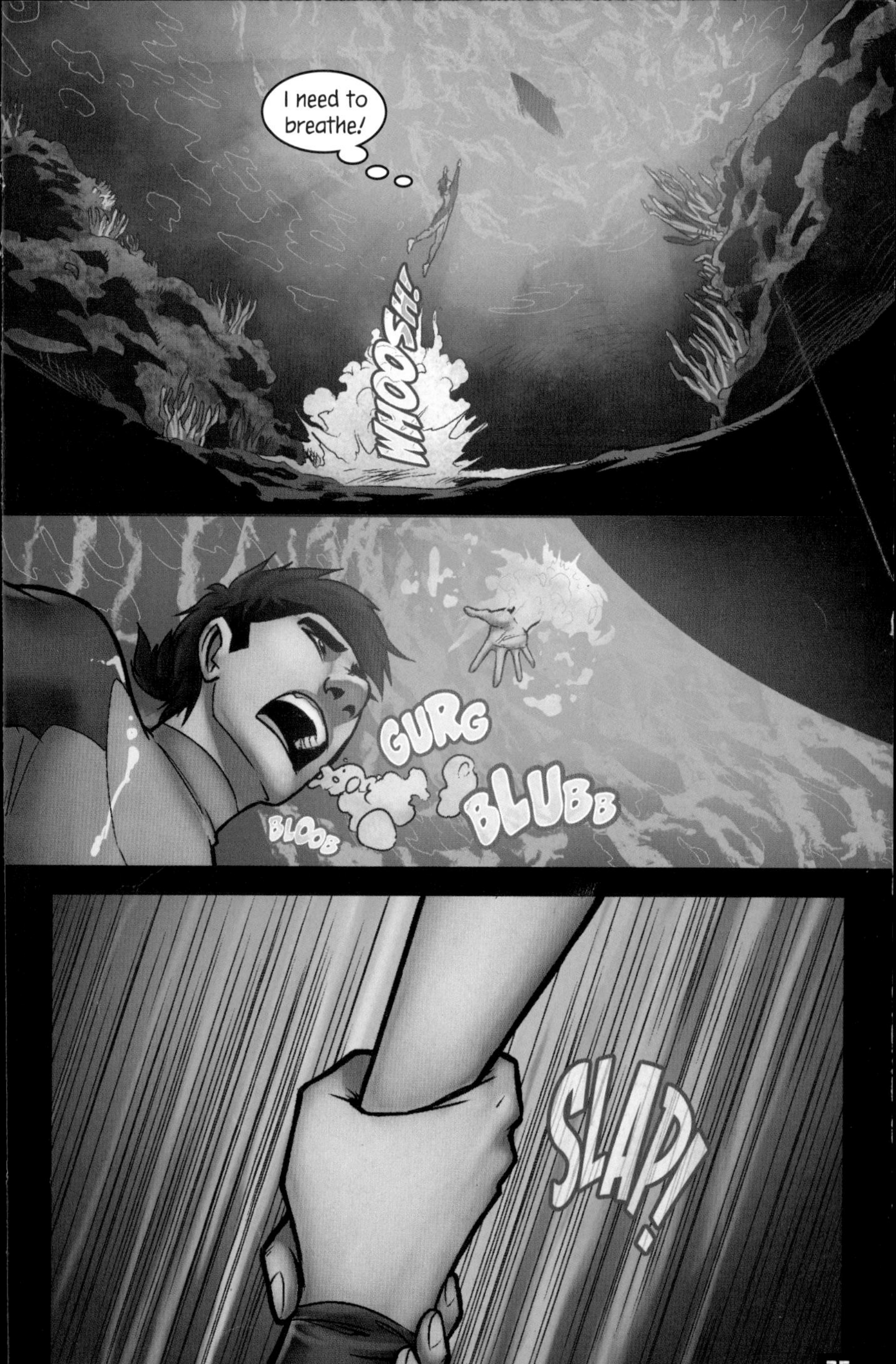
I need to breathe!
WHOOSH!
GURG
BLOOB
BLUBB
SLAP!

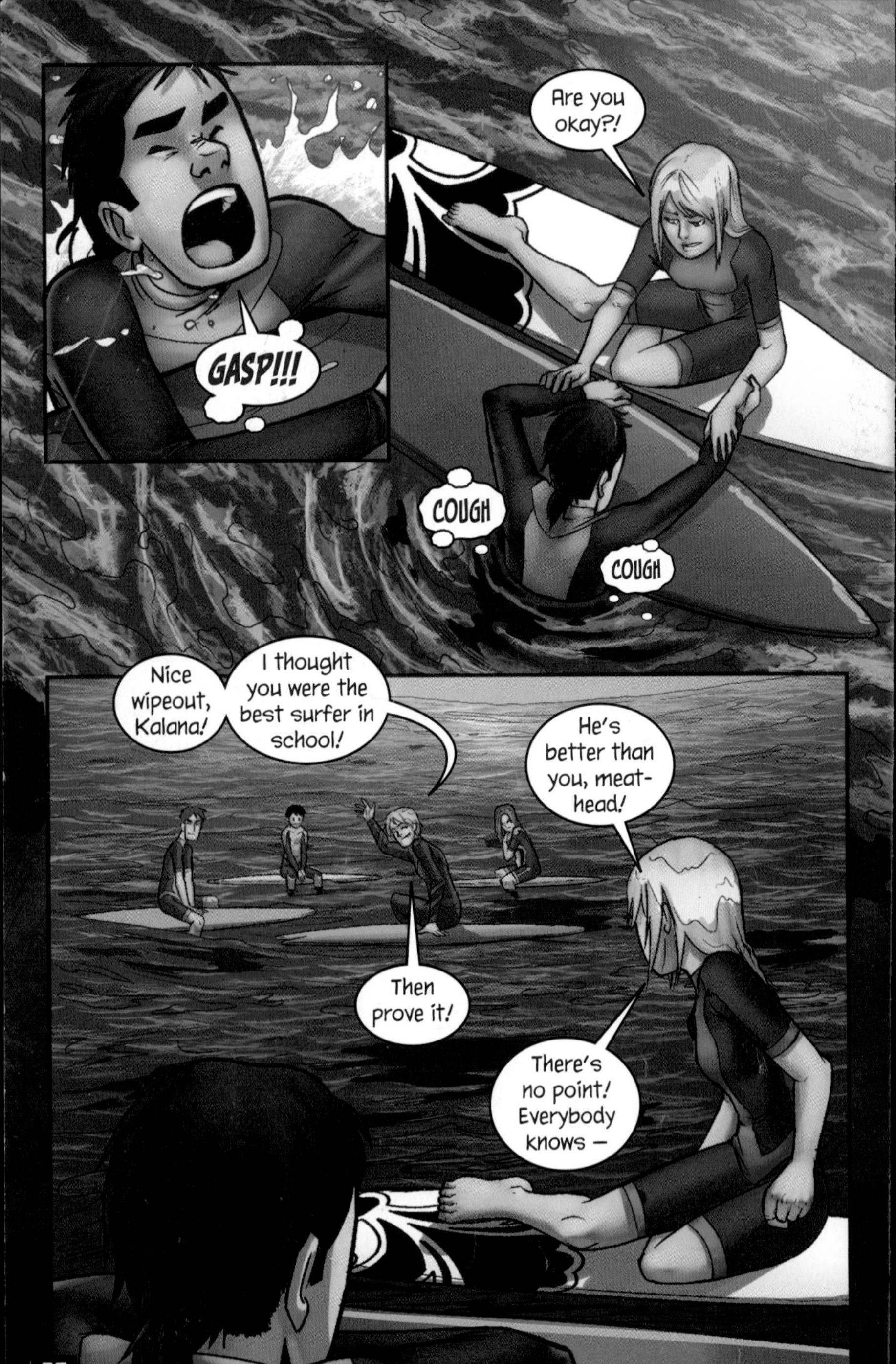
GASP!!!
Are you okay?!
COUGH
COUGH
Nice wipeout, Kalana!
I thought you were the best surfer in school!
He's better than you, meat-head!
Then prove it!
There's no point! Everybody knows —

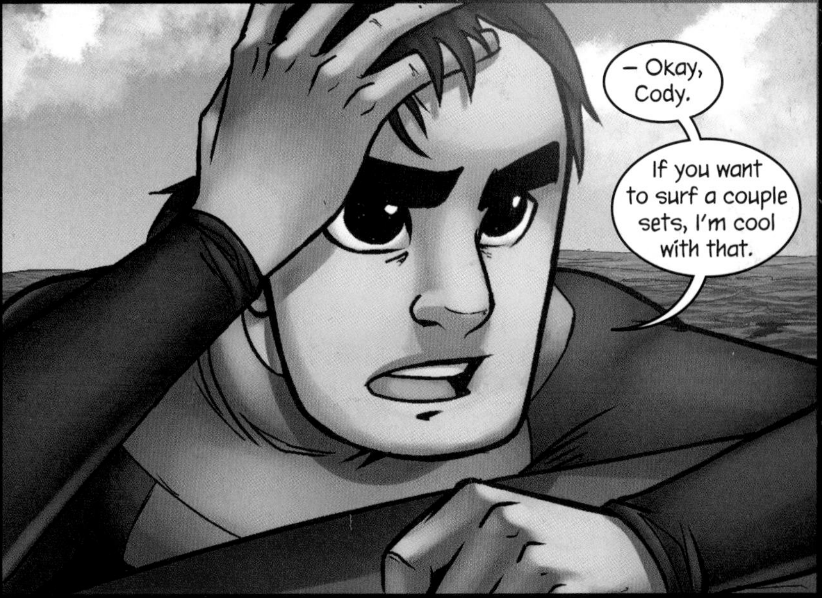
– Okay, Cody.
If you want to surf a couple sets, I'm cool with that.

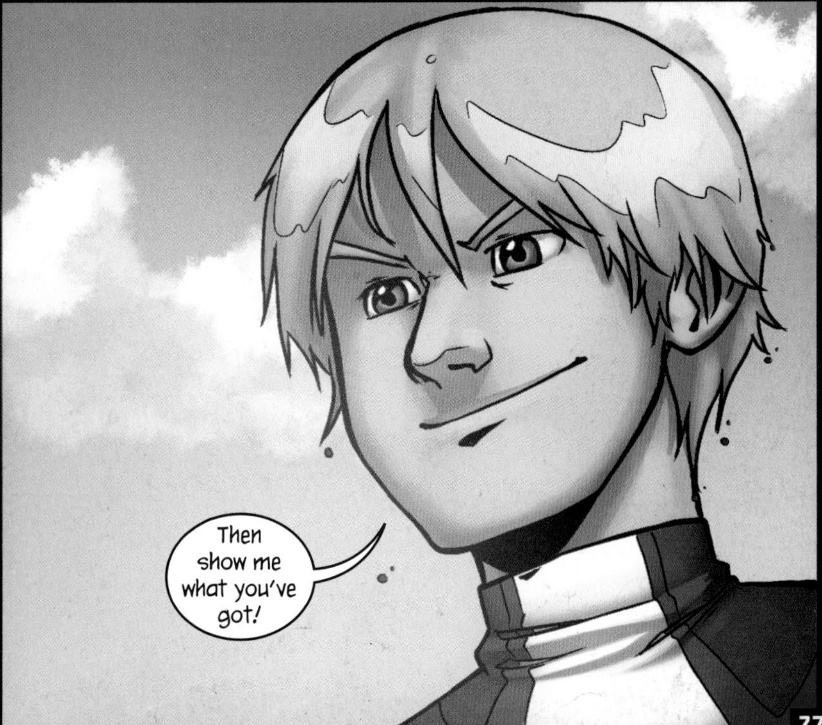
Then show me what you've got!

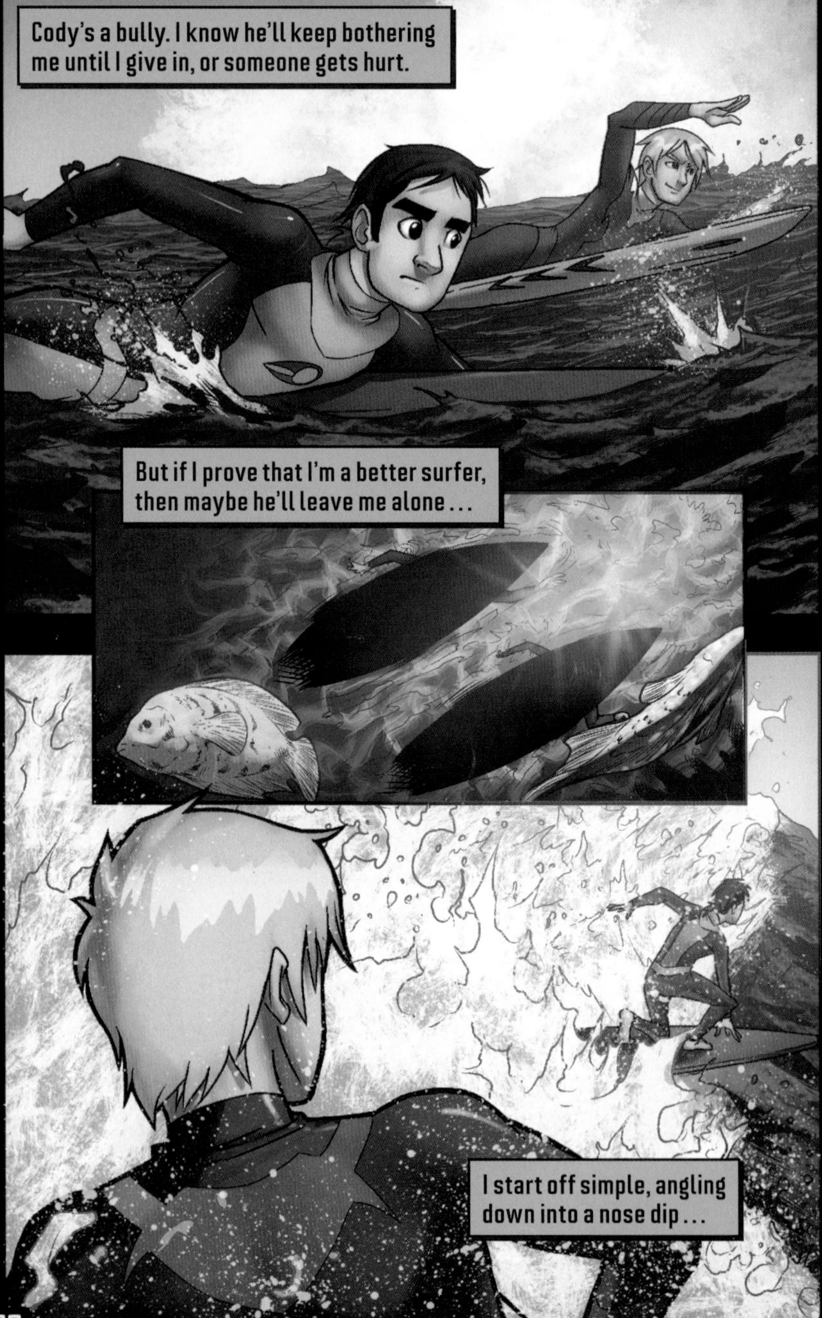

Cody's a bully. I know he'll keep bothering me until I give in, or someone gets hurt.
But if I prove that I'm a better surfer, then maybe he'll leave me alone . . .
I start off simple, angling down into a nose dip . . .

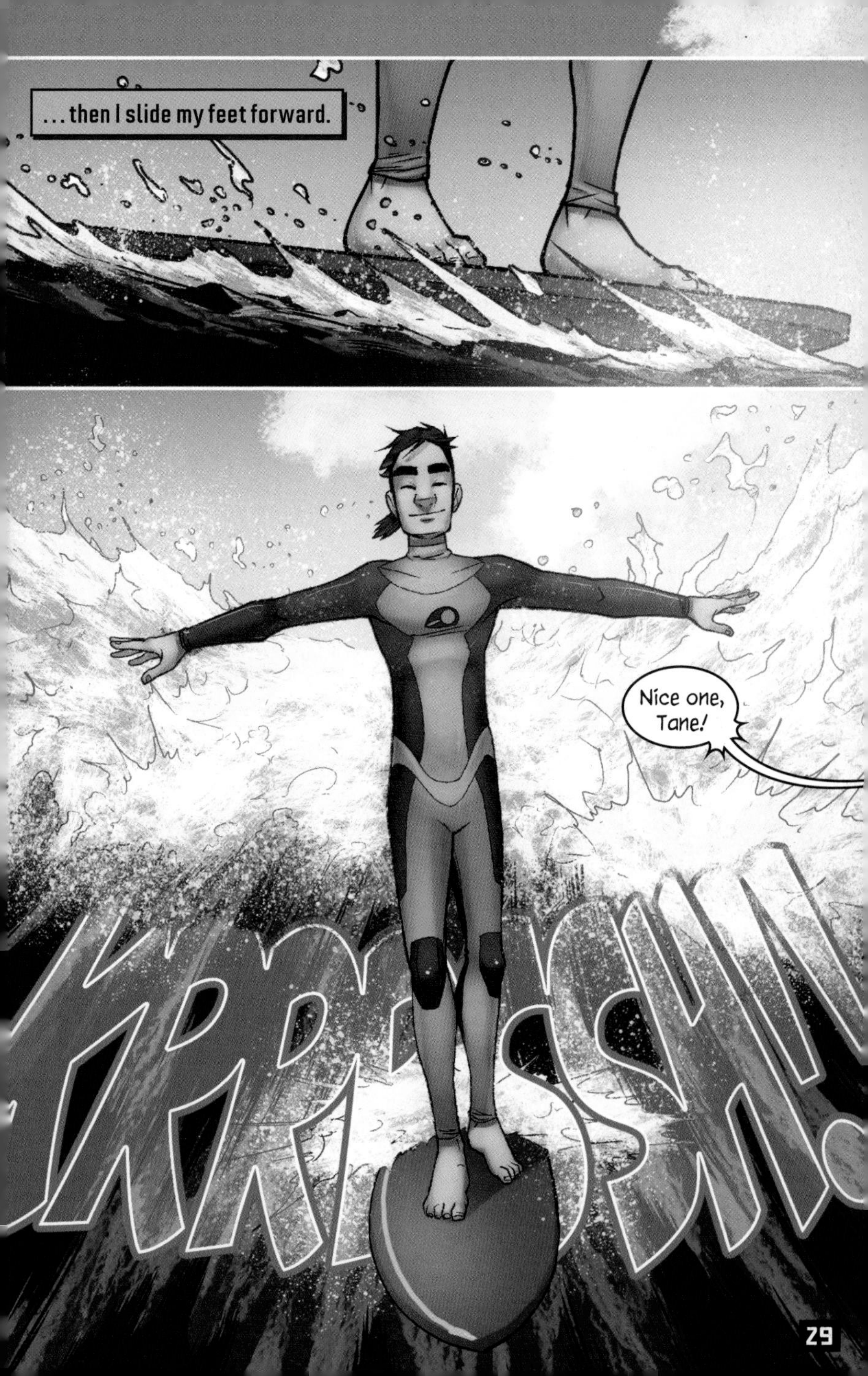
. . . then I slide my feet forward.
Nice one, Tane!

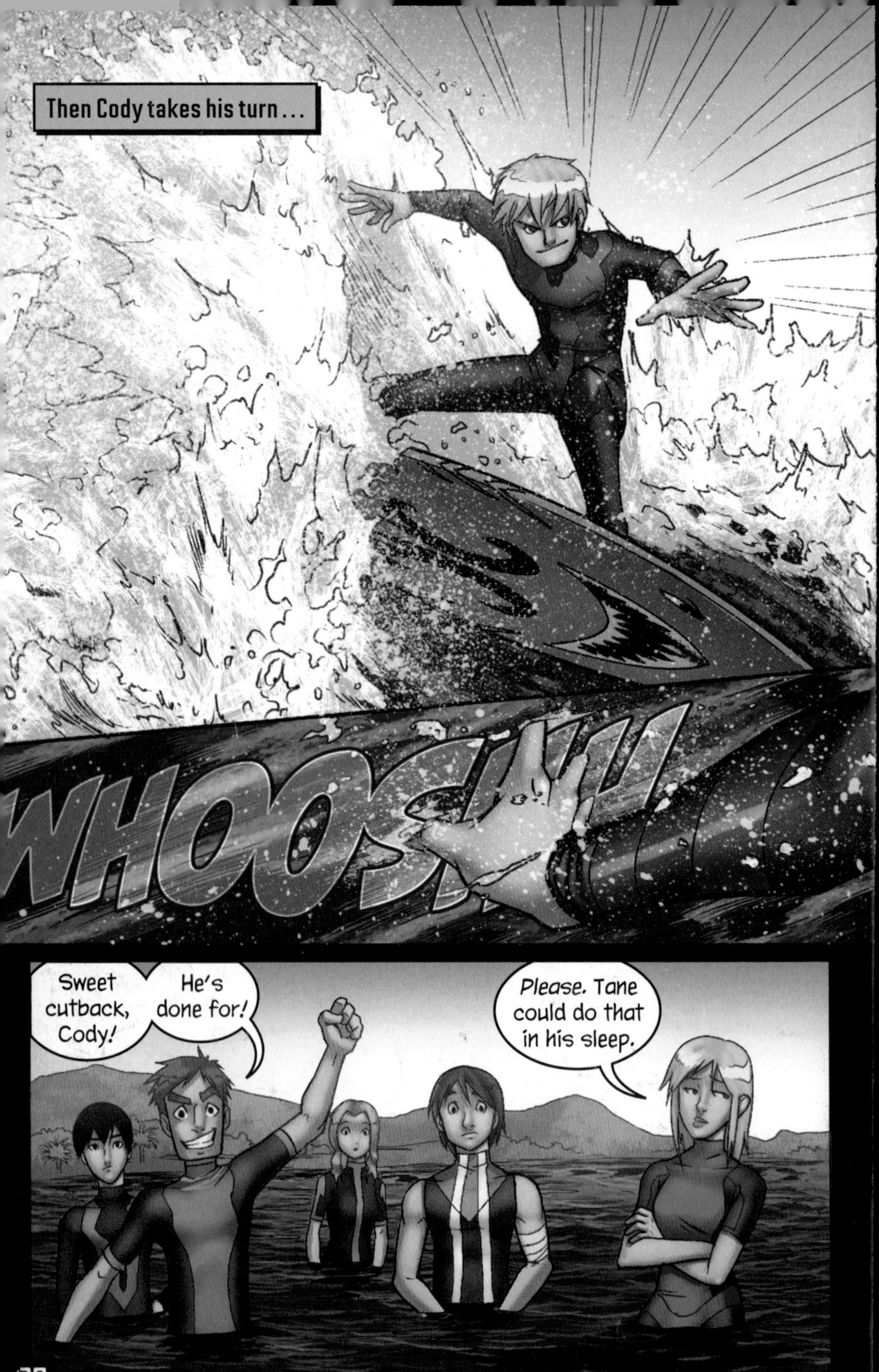
Then Cody takes his turn . . .
WHOOSH!!
Sweet cutback, Cody!
He's done for!
Please. Tane could do that in his sleep.

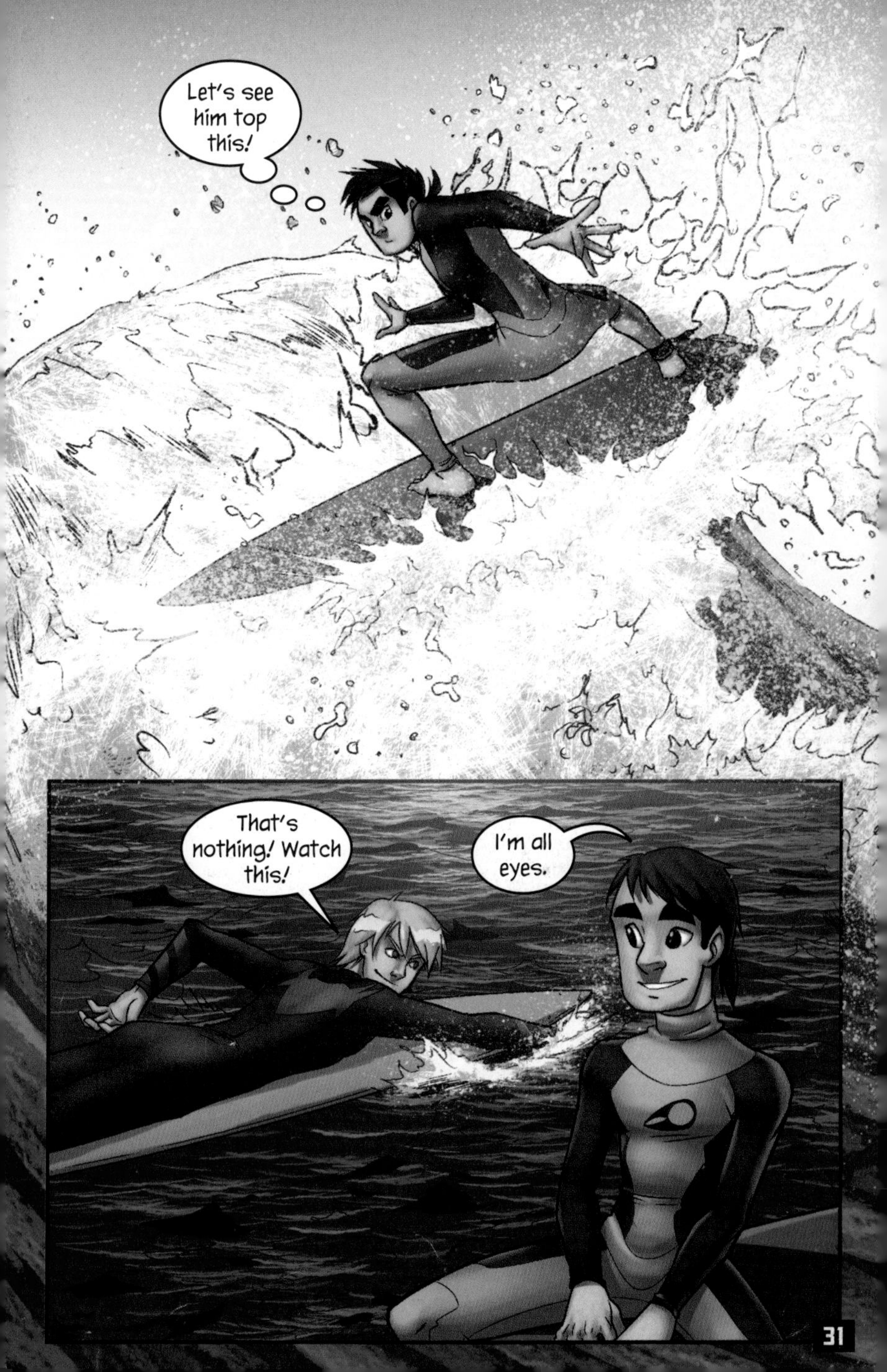
Let's see him top this!
That's nothing! Watch this!
I'm all eyes.

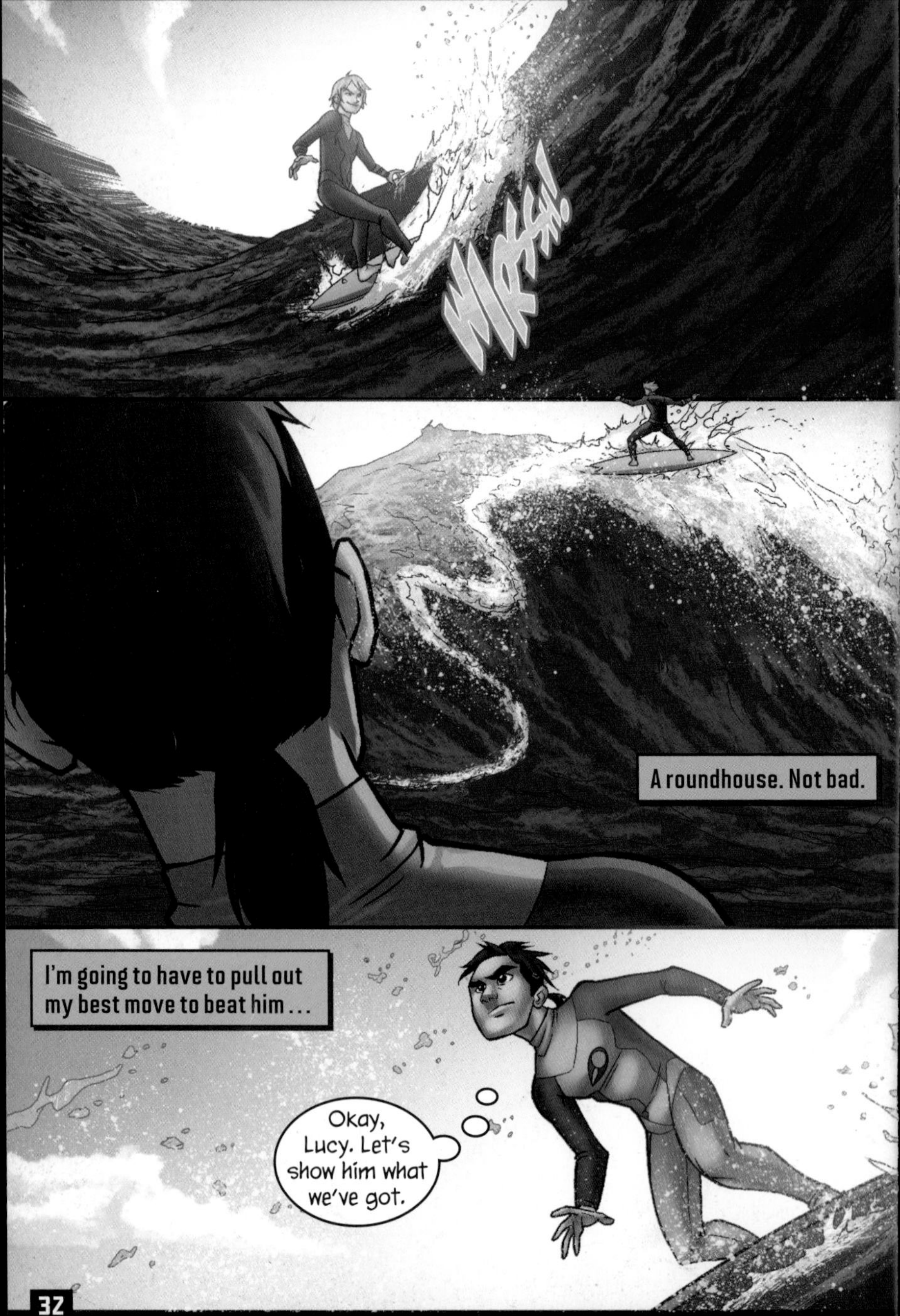
A roundhouse. Not bad.
I'm going to have to pull out my best move to beat him . . .
Okay, Lucy. Let's show him what we've got.

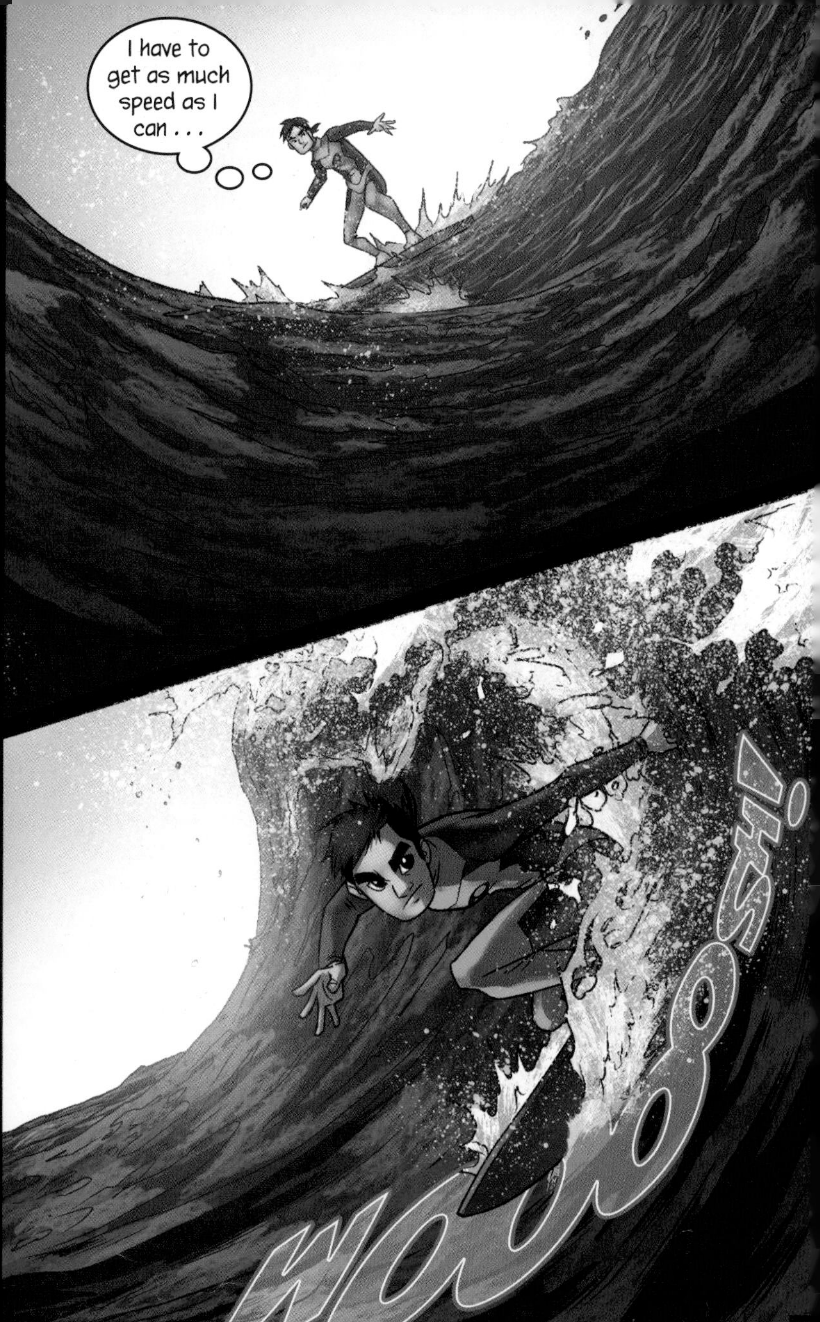
I have to get as much speed as I can . . .
WHOOOSH!

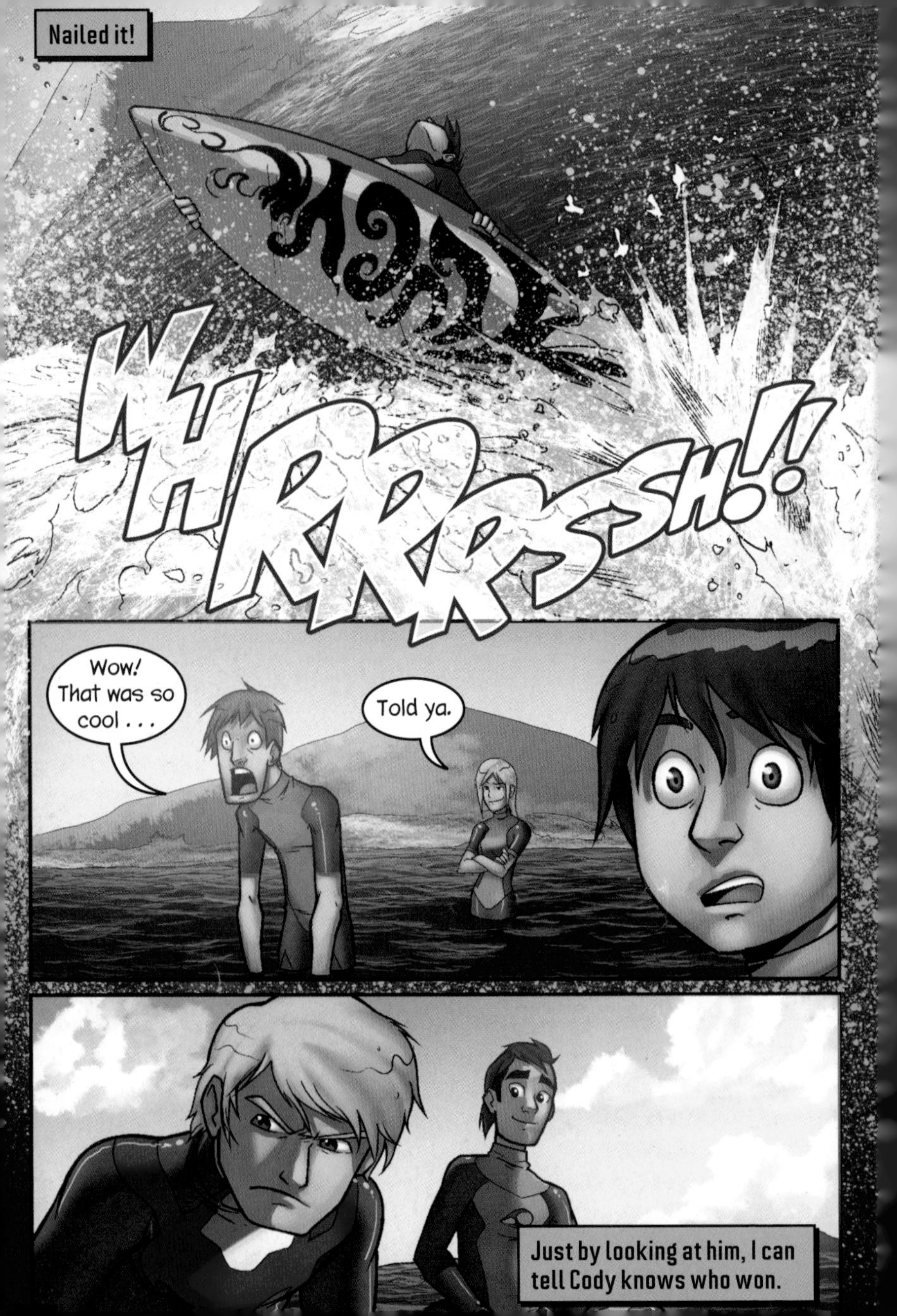

Nailed it!
WHRRRSSH!!
Wow! That was so cool . . .
Told ya.
Just by looking at him, I can tell Cody knows who won.

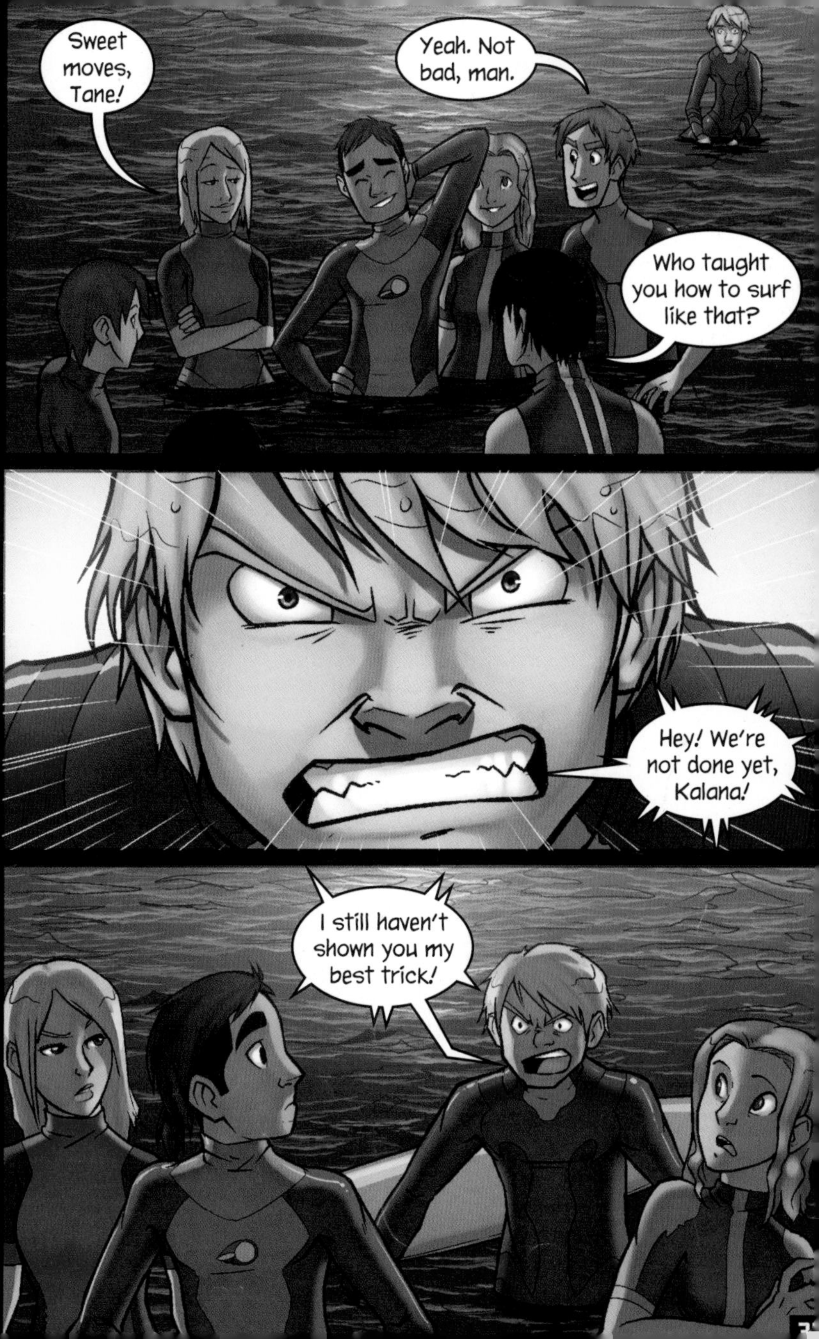
Sweet moves, Tane!
Yeah. Not bad, man.
Who taught you how to surf like that?
Hey! We're not done yet, Kalana!
I still haven't shown you my best trick!

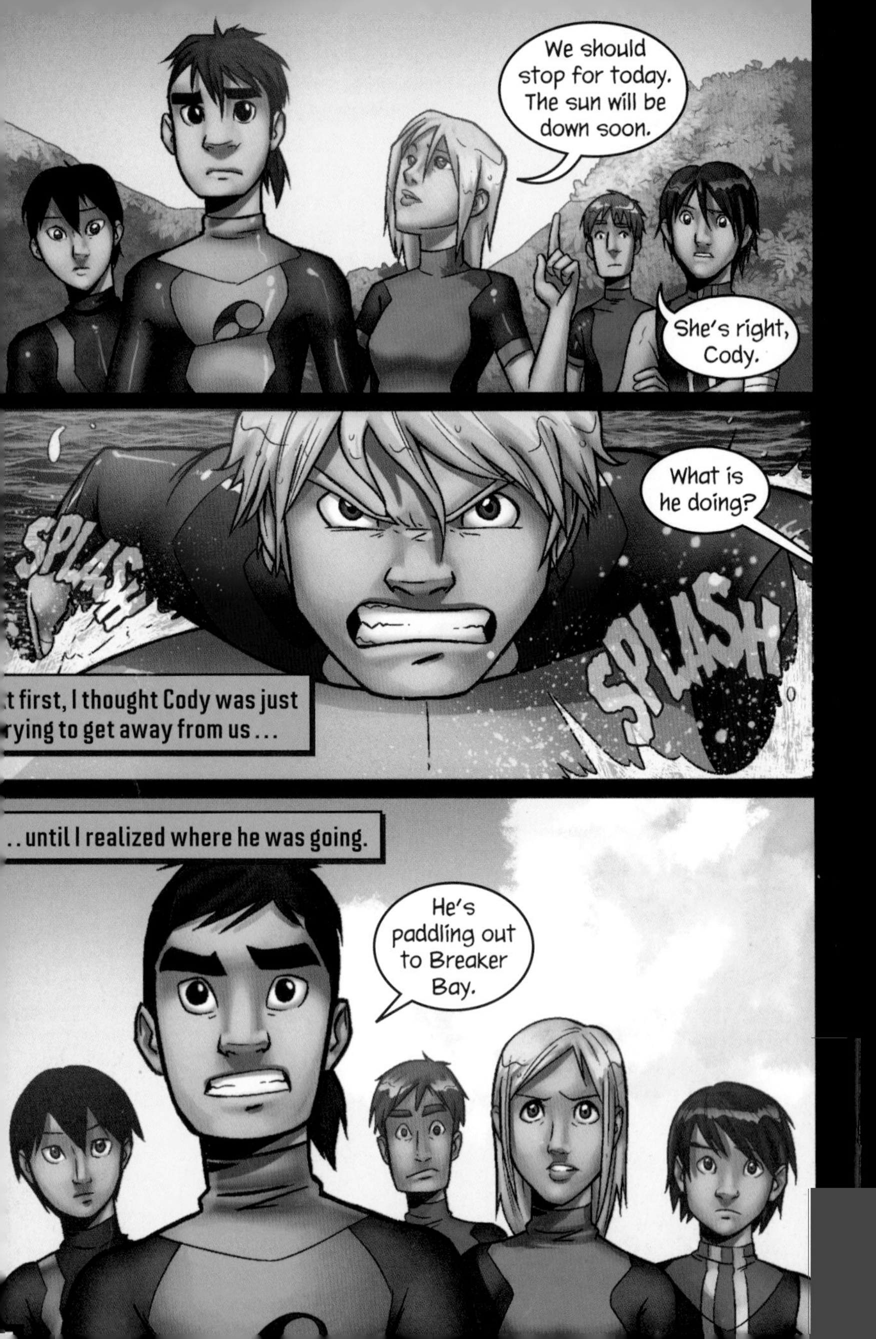

We should stop for today. The sun will be down soon.
She's right, Cody.
What is he doing?
SPLASH
SPLASH
t first, I thought Cody was just rying to get away from us . . .
. . until I realized where he was going.
He's paddling out to Breaker Bay.

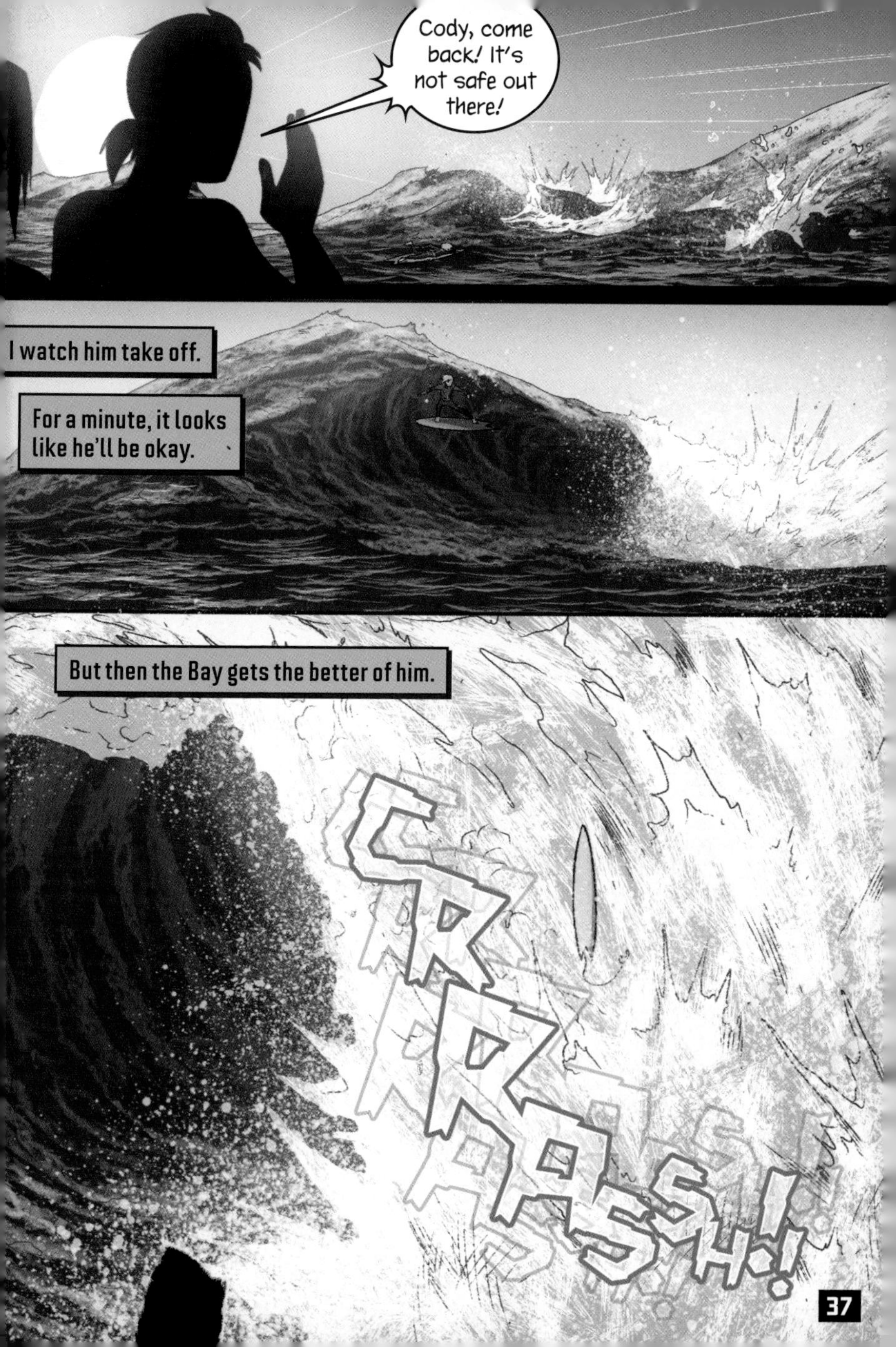
Cody, come back! It's not safe out there!
I watch him take off.
For a minute, it looks like he'll be okay.
But then the Bay gets the better of him.
CRASH!

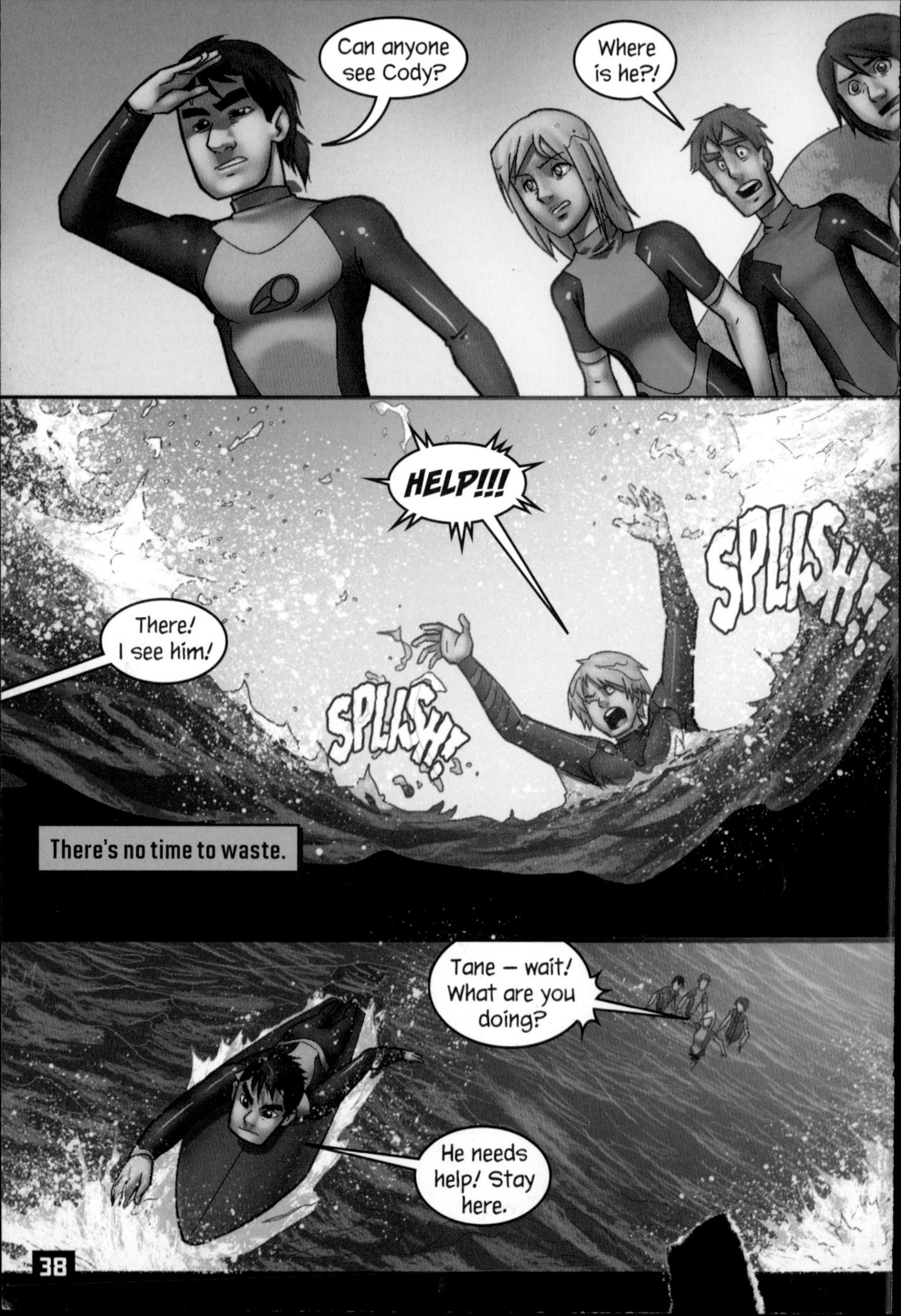

Can anyone see Cody?
Where is he?!
HELP!!!
SPLISH!!
There! I see him!
SPLISH!!
There's no time to waste.
Tane — wait! What are you doing?
He needs help! Stay here.

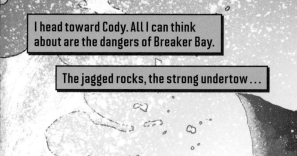

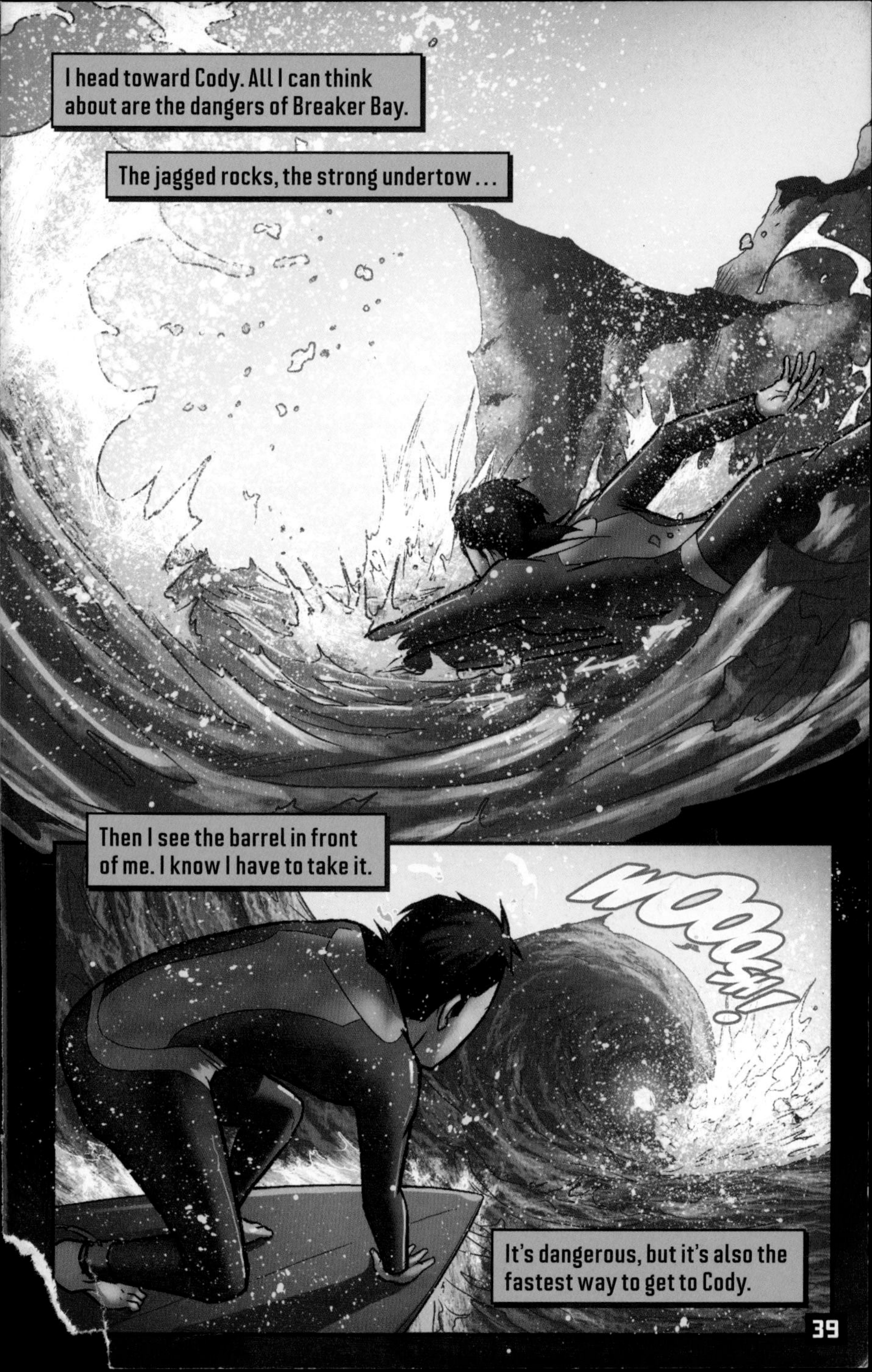

I head toward Cody. All I can think about are the dangers of Breaker Bay.

The jagged rocks, the strong undertow ...

Then I see the barrel in front of me. I know I have to take it.

WOOOSH!

It's dangerous, but it's also the fastest way to get to Cody.

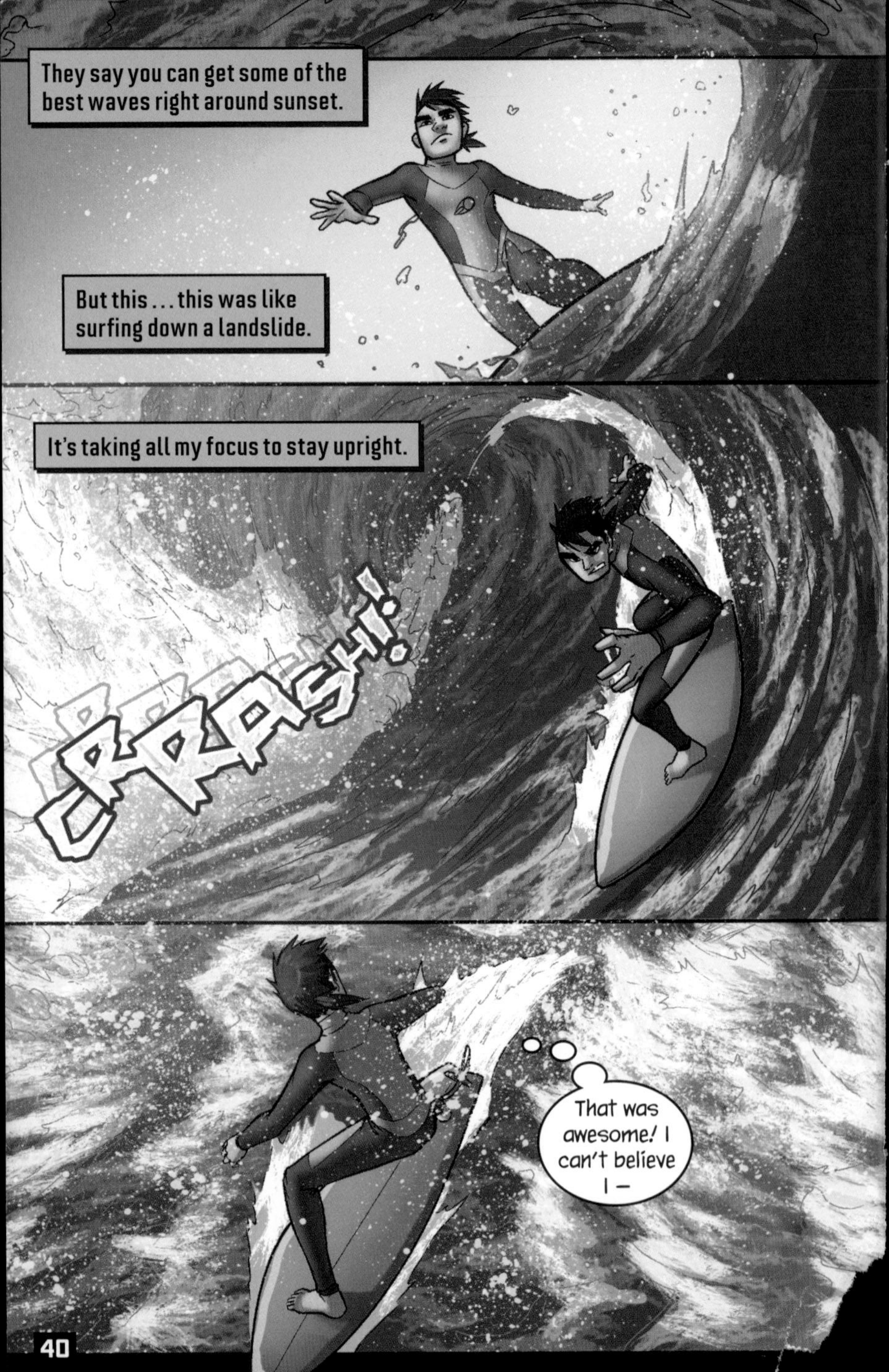
They say you can get some of the best waves right around sunset.
But this . . . this was like surfing down a landslide.
It's taking all my focus to stay upright.
CRASH!
That was awesome! I can't believe I —

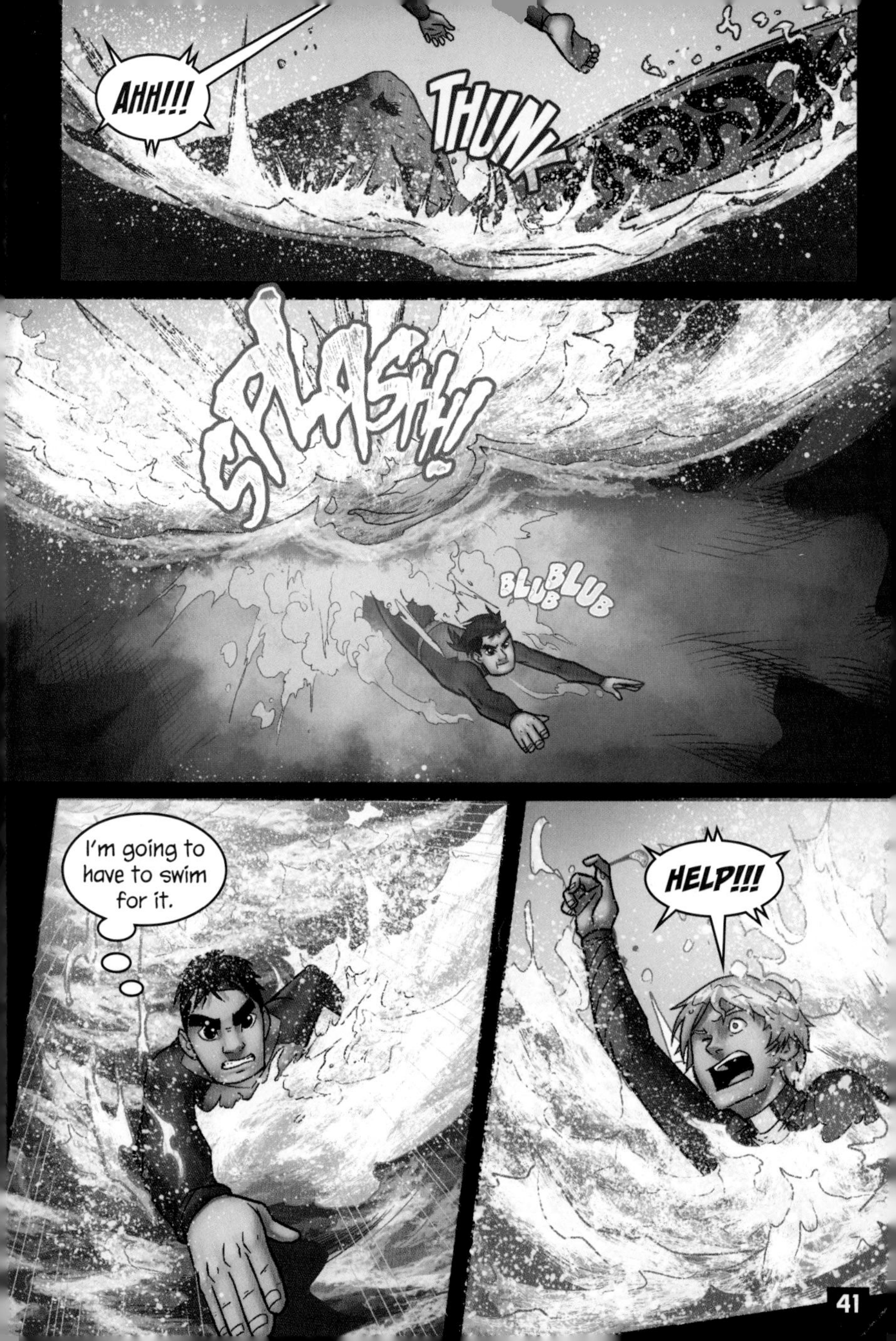
AHH!!!
THUNK
SPLASH!!
BLUB BLUB BLUB
I'm going to have to swim for it.
HELP!!!

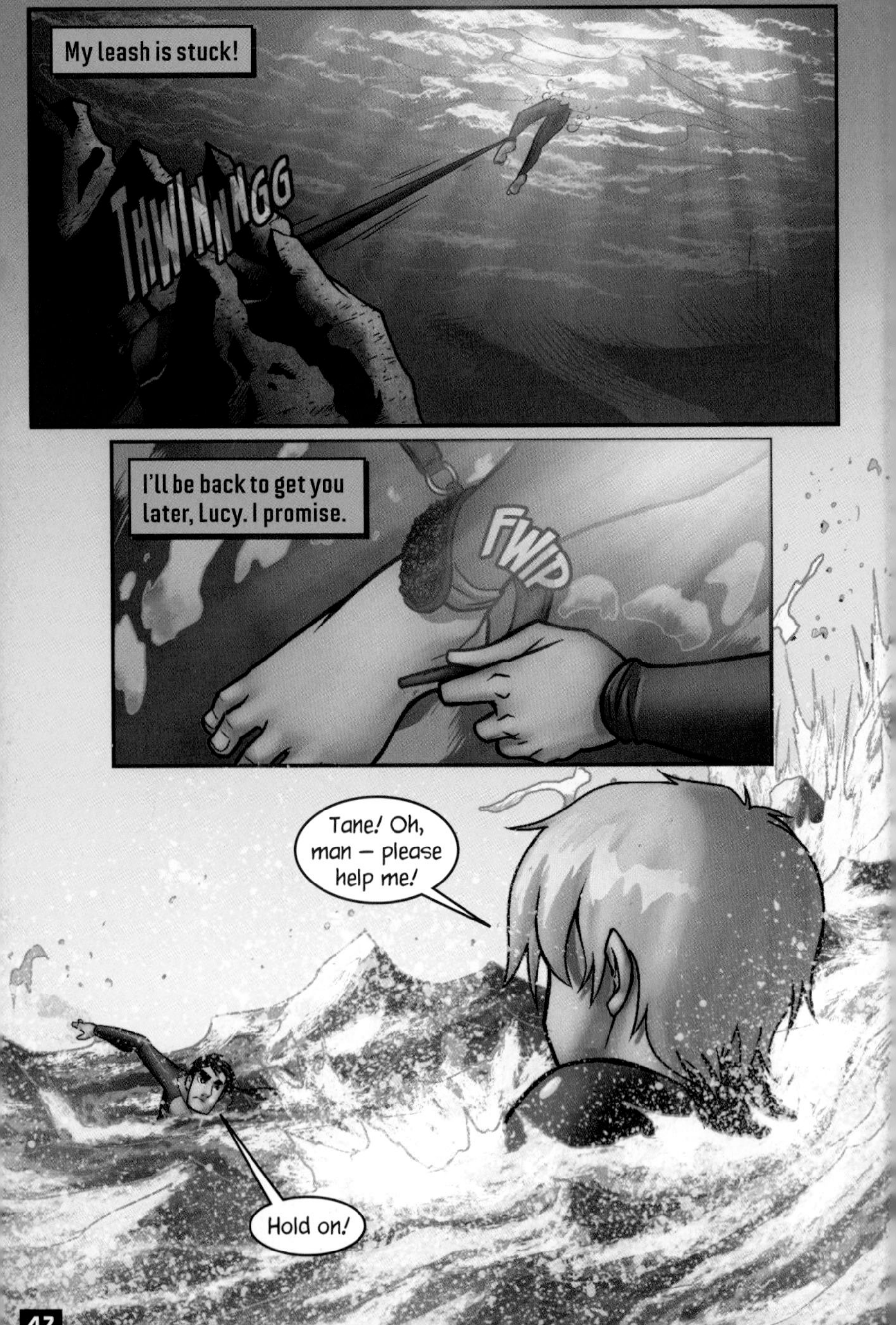
My leash is stuck!
THWINNNGG
I'll be back to get you later, Lucy. I promise.
FWIP
Tane! Oh, man — please help me!
Hold on!

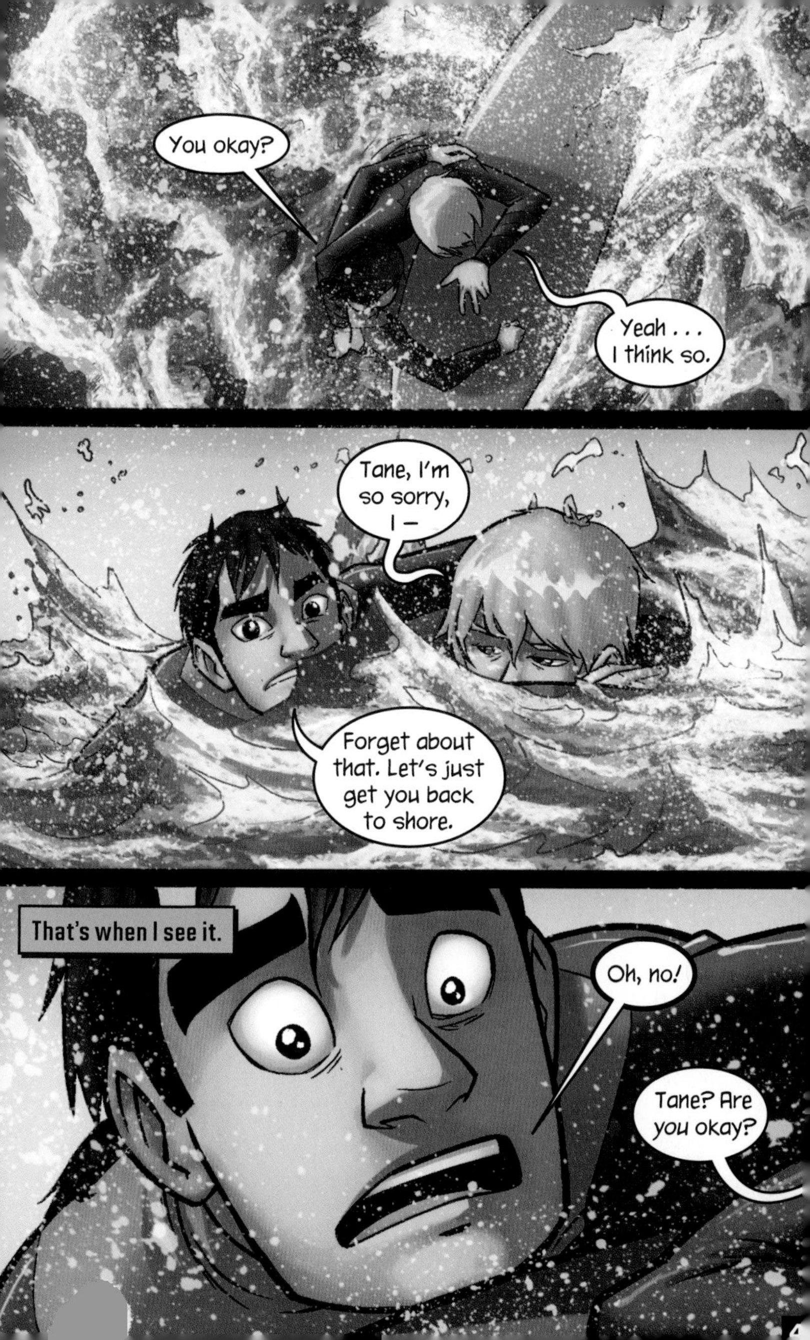
You okay?
Yeah . . . I think so.
Tane, I'm so sorry, I —
Forget about that. Let's just get you back to shore.
That's when I see it.
Oh, no!
Tane? Are you okay?

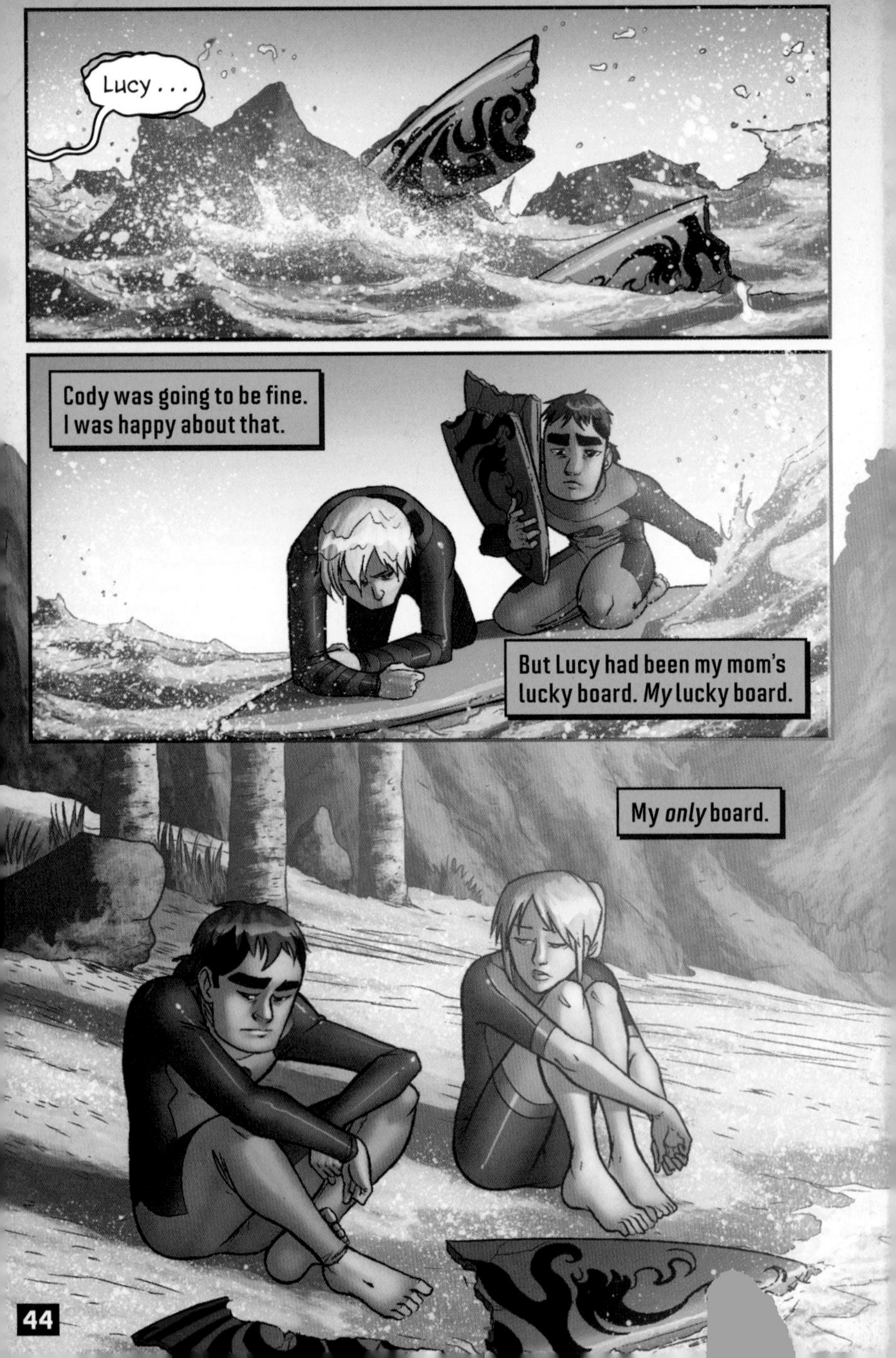
Lucy . . .
Cody was going to be fine. I was happy about that.
But Lucy had been my mom's lucky board. *My* lucky board.
My *only* board.

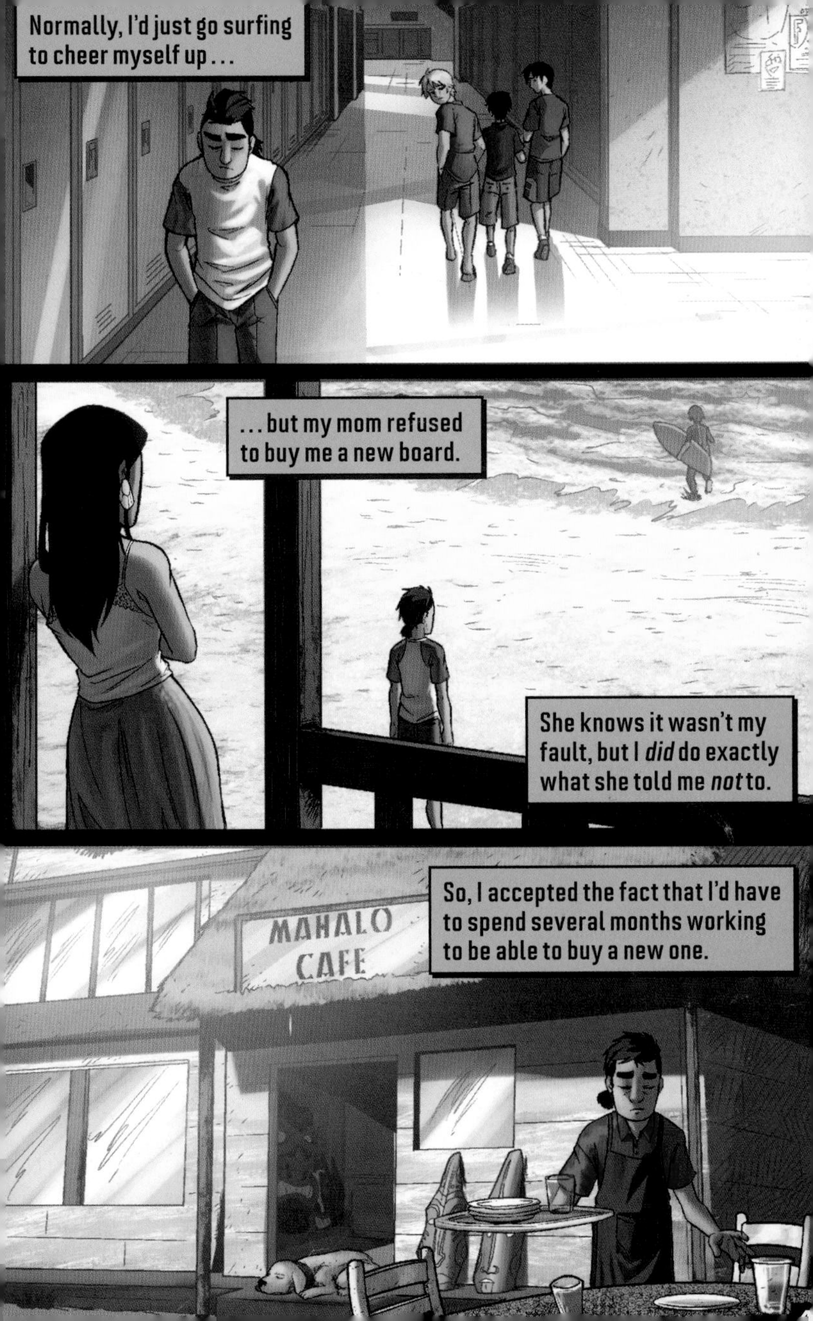

Normally, I'd just go surfing to cheer myself up . . .
. . . but my mom refused to buy me a new board.
She knows it wasn't my fault, but I *did* do exactly what she told me *not* to.
So, I accepted the fact that I'd have to spend several months working to be able to buy a new one.
MAHALO CAFE

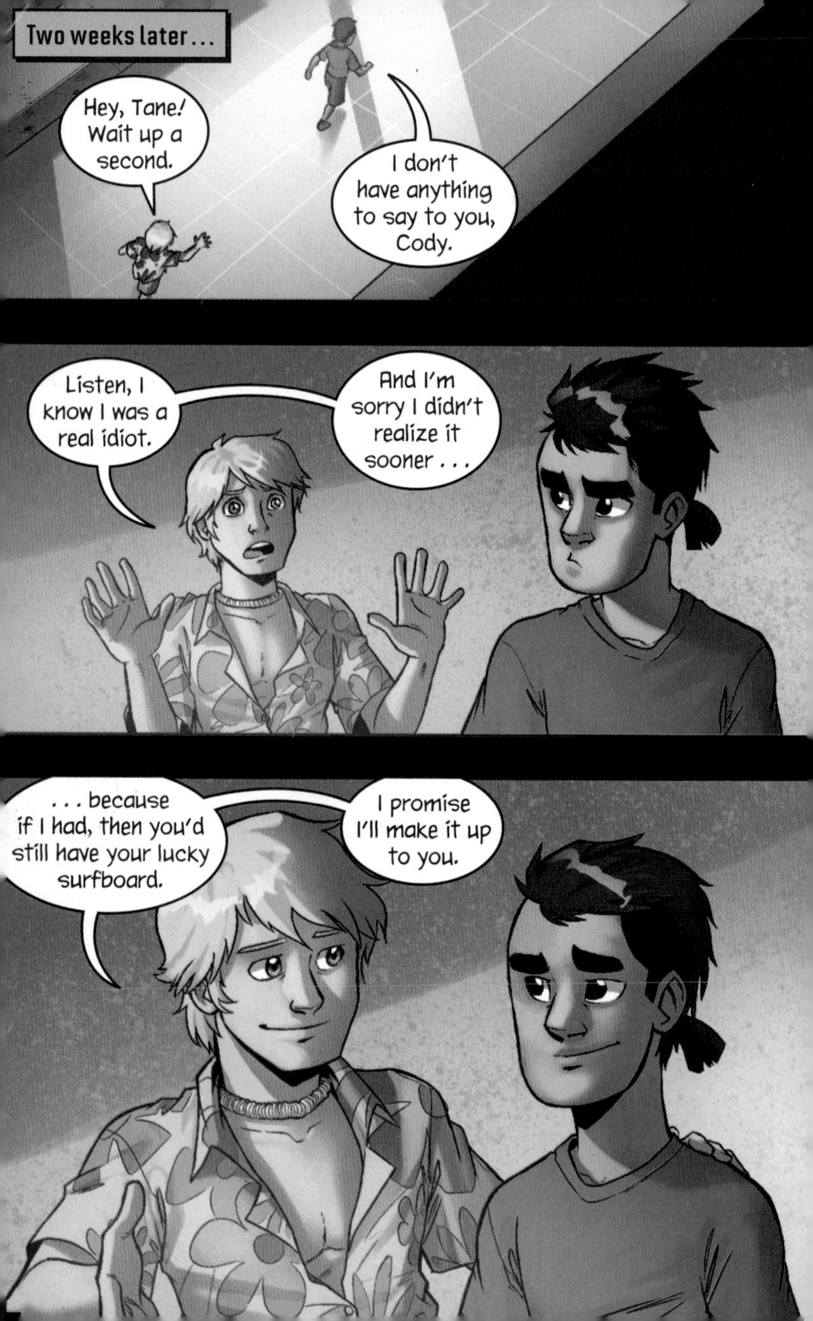
Two weeks later . . .
Hey, Tane! Wait up a second.
I don't have anything to say to you, Cody.
Listen, I know I was a real idiot.
And I'm sorry I didn't realize it sooner . . .
. . . because if I had, then you'd still have your lucky surfboard.
I promise I'll make it up to you.

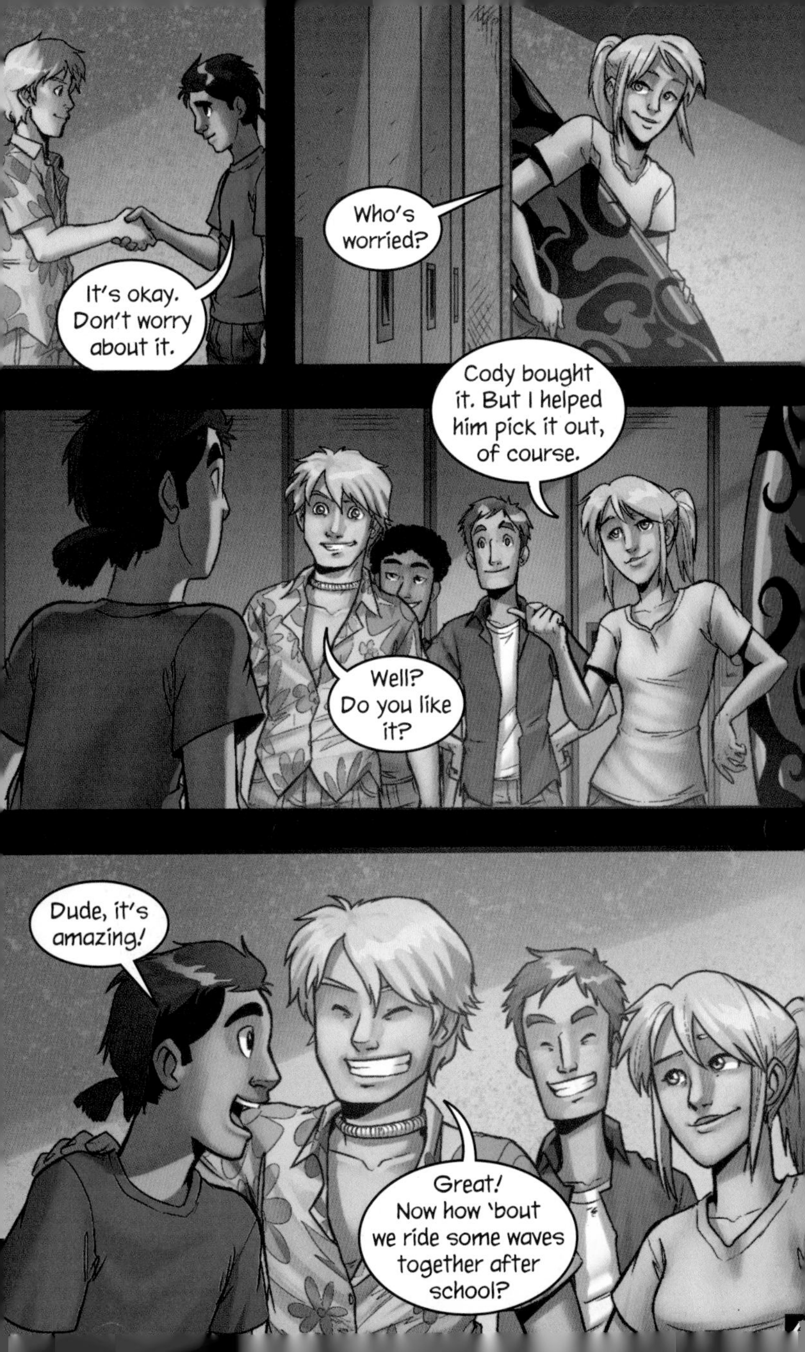
It's okay. Don't worry about it.
Who's worried?
Cody bought it. But I helped him pick it out, of course.
Well? Do you like it?
Dude, it's amazing!
Great! Now how 'bout we ride some waves together after school?

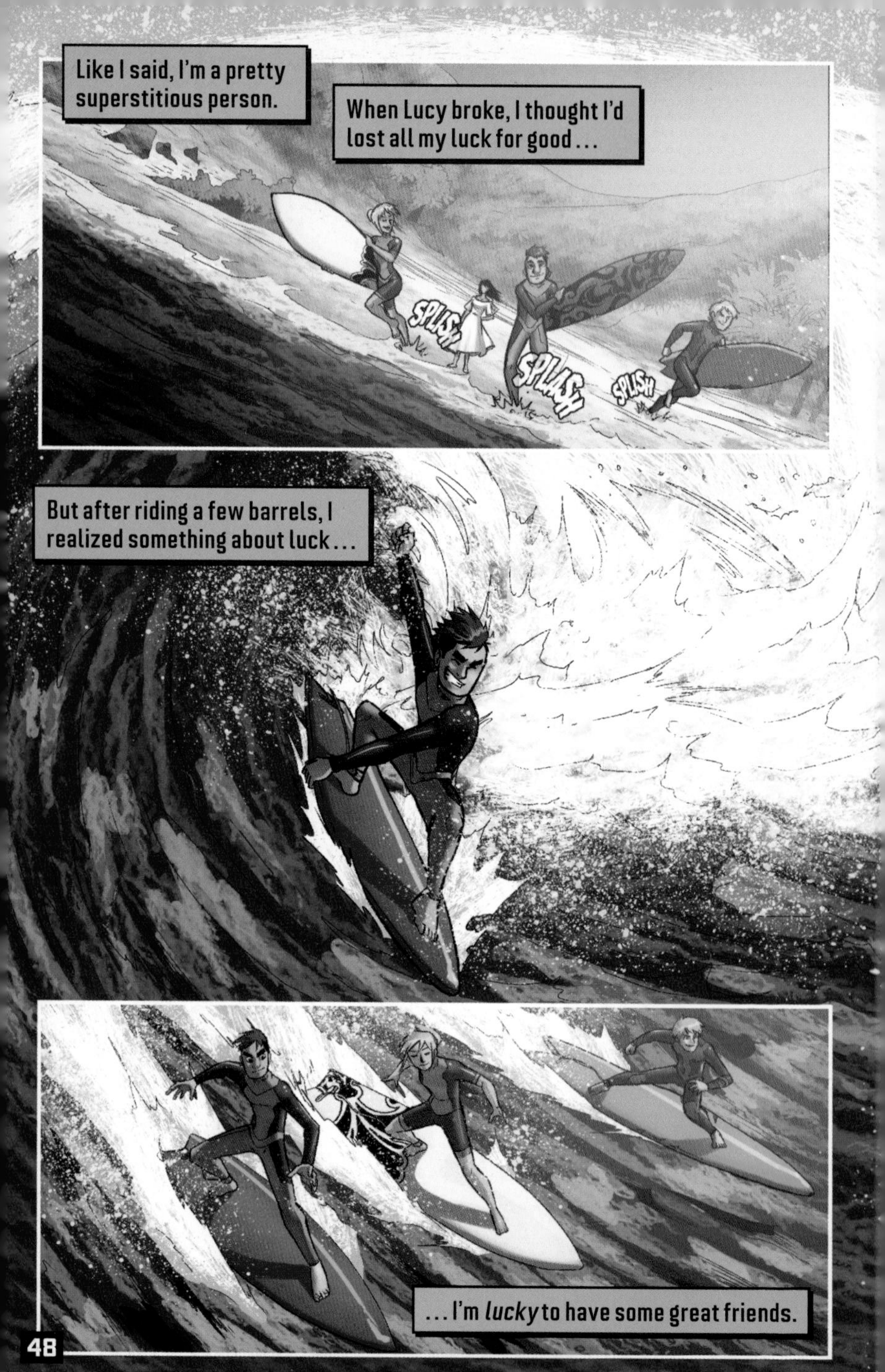
Like I said, I'm a pretty superstitious person.
When Lucy broke, I thought I'd lost all my luck for good . . .
SPLISH
SPLASH
SPLISH
But after riding a few barrels, I realized something about luck . . .
. . . I'm *lucky* to have some great friends.

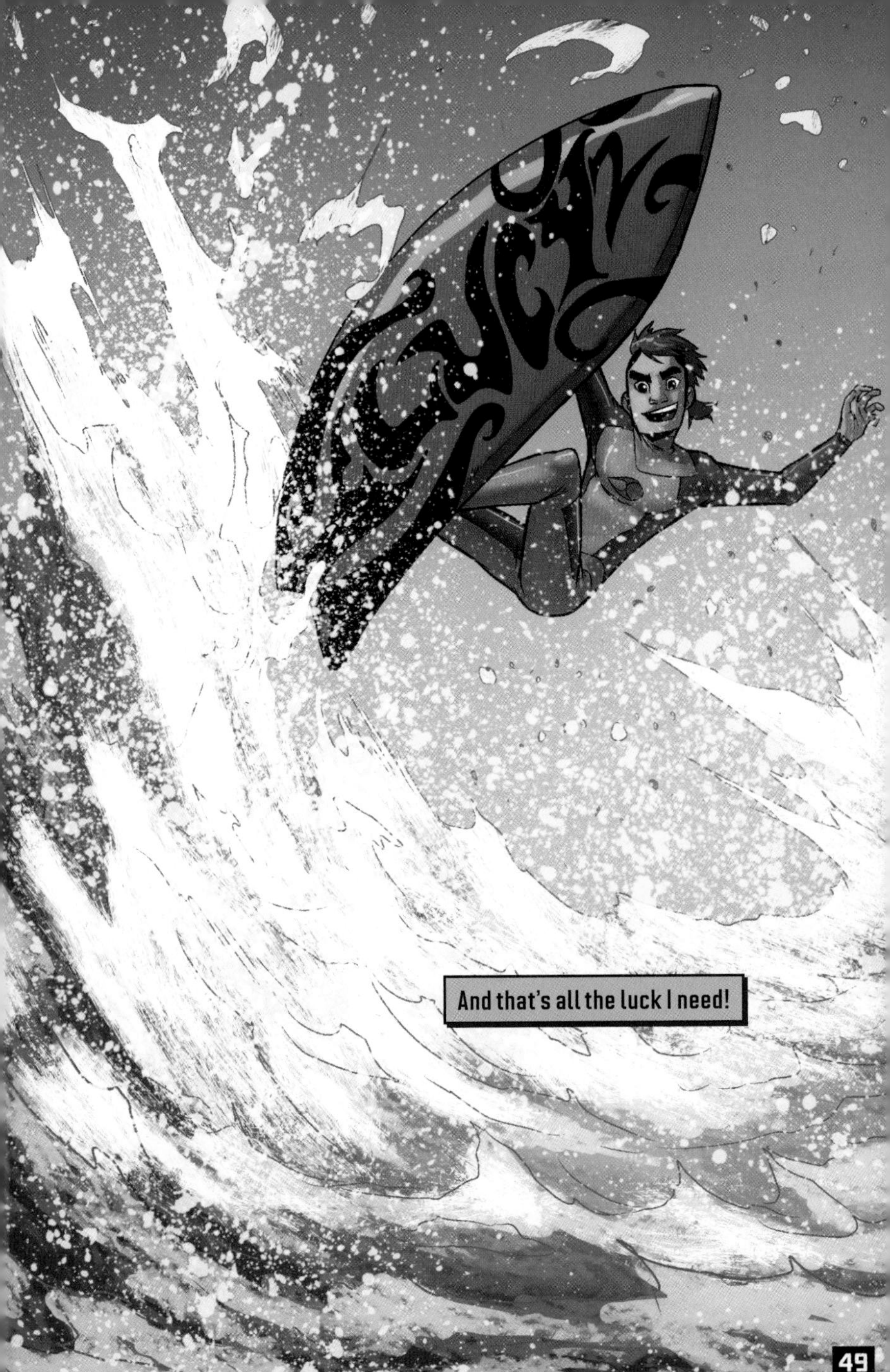
And that's all the luck I need!

F

BROKEN SURFBOARD LEADS TO NEW FRIENDSHIP

STORY: Cody's ill-advised attempt to surf the wild waves of Breaker Bay led to the destruction of Tane's surfboard, Lucy. However, Tane says that his new board more than makes up for Cody's big mistake. "It was kind of a good thing it happened, actually," Tane says. "For one thing, I realized it wasn't just luck that made me good. And for another, I made a new friend in the process!"

POWERED BY **STONE ARCH**

BLZ vs BMS
3-1
TGR vs ROK
33-32
EAG vs BA
14-7
SPA vs WE
4-3
BAN vs RO
21-15
R2R vs LIG
4-3
BLZ vs
3-1

SZ POSTGAME EXTRA

WHERE *YOU* ANALYZE THE GAME!

> Surfing fans got a real treat today when Tane Kalana one-upped his surfing bully and made a new friend in the process. Let's go into the stands and ask some fans for their opinions on the day's exciting conclusion...

DISCUSSION QUESTION 1

What are some other ways Tane could have gotten Cody to stop bullying him? Talk about some ways that kids can stop bullies without fighting.

DISCUSSION QUESTION 2

Cody and Tane surf at Breaker Bay despite being told not to. What kinds of things have you done that got you in trouble? Talk about it.

WRITING PROMPT 1

Imagine that you were given your own custom-made surfboard. Write a basic description of the board, then draw a picture of it.

WRITING PROMPT 2

Is Tane a hero for saving Cody like he did? What is your definition of a hero? Have you ever done anything you thought was heroic? Write about it.

(BAYL)—jump off a moving object

(BA-ruhl)—the inside part of a wave that is hollow. It is also known as a "tube."

(FATE)—what will happen to you

(MOK-ing)—making fun of someone

(NUR-vuhss)—easily upset or tense

(ROUND-houss)—a surfing trick that involves a full or half rotation

(soo-pur-STI-shuhss)—if you are superstitious, you believe that good and bad luck can affect you

(TEMPT-ing)—to appeal strongly to, or attract

CREATORS

Brandon Terrell › Author

Brandon Terrell is a writer and filmmaker who has worked in the Minnesota film and television community for nearly ten years. He is the author of the graphic novel *Horrorwood*, published by Ape Entertainment. He is also an avid baseball fan, and is crazy about the Minnesota Twins. Terrell lives in Saint Paul with his wife, Jennifer.

Andres Esparza › Inker

Andres Esparza has been a graphic designer, colorist, and illustrator for many different companies and agencies. Andres now works as a full-time artist for Graphikslava studio in Monterrey, Mexico. In his spare time, Andres loves to play basketball, hang out with family and friends, and listen to good music.

Fernando Cano › Penciler & Colorist

Fernando Cano is an emerging illustrator born in Mexico City, Mexico. He currently resides in Monterrey, Mexico, where he works as a full-time illustrator and colorist at Graphikslava studio. He has done illustration work for Marvel, DC Comics, and role-playing games like Pathfinder from Paizo Publishing. In his spare time, he enjoys hanging out with friends, singing, rowing, and drawing!

GRAPHIC NOVELS KIDS

QUICK COMIC

SKATEBOARD BREAKDOWN

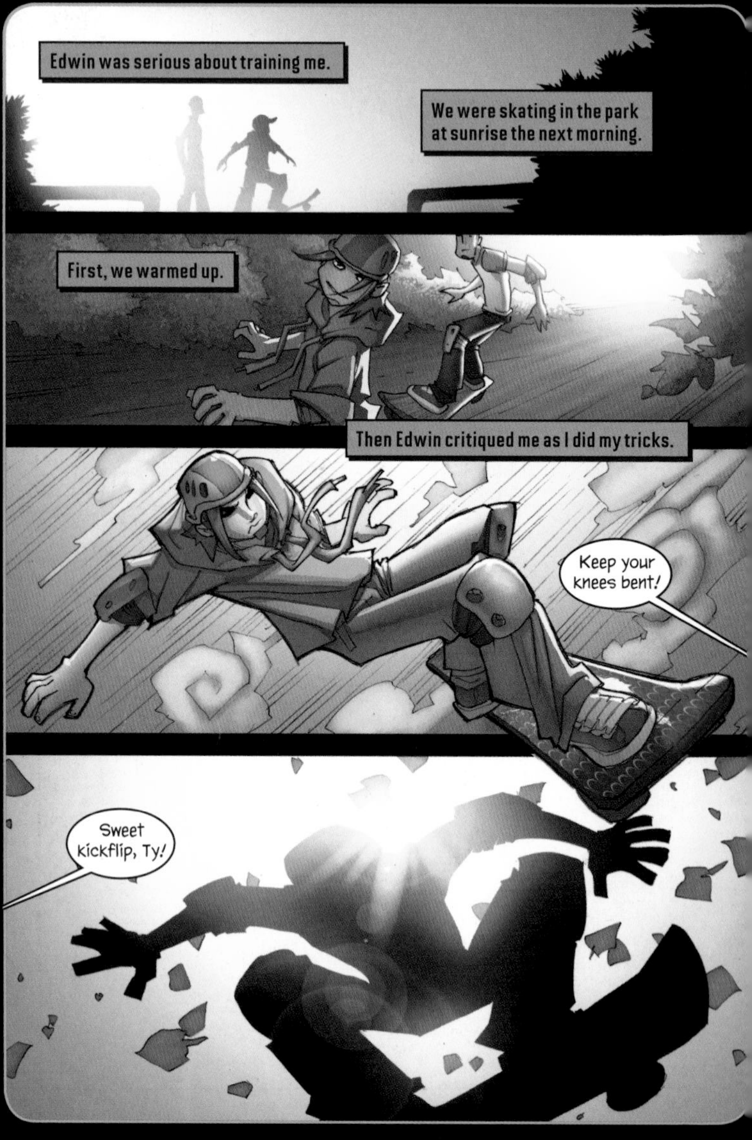
Edwin was serious about training me.
We were skating in the park at sunrise the next morning.
First, we warmed up.
Then Edwin critiqued me as I did my tricks.
Keep your knees bent!
Sweet kickflip, Ty!

HOT SPORTS. HOT FORMAT!

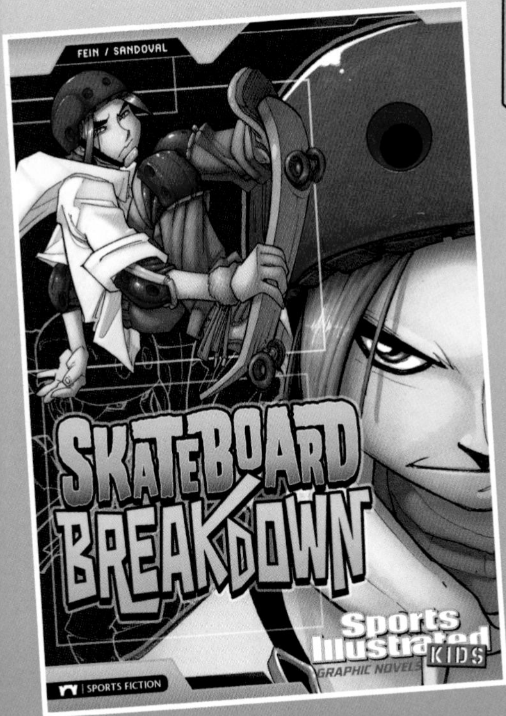
FEIN / SANDOVAL
SKATEBOARD BREAKDOWN
Sports Illustrated KIDS
GRAPHIC NOVELS
SPORTS FICTION

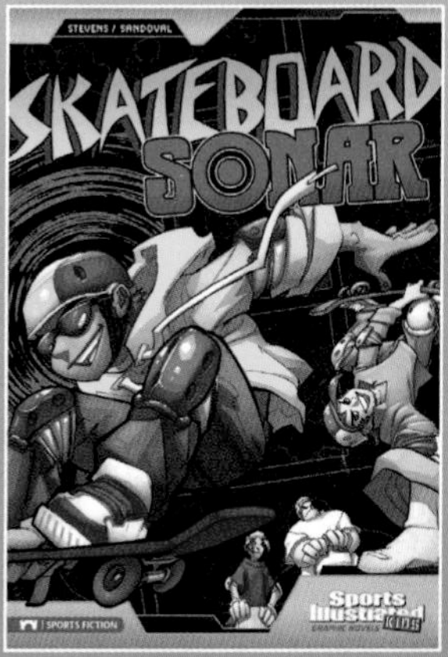
STEVENS / SANDOVAL
SKATEBOARD SONAR
SPORTS FICTION
Sports Illustrated KIDS
GRAPHIC NOVELS

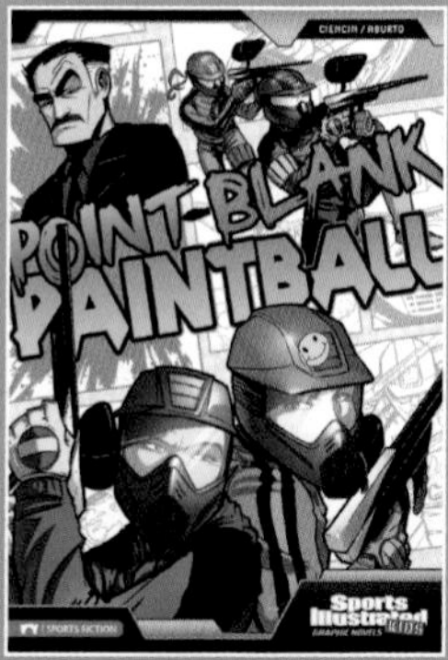
CIENCIN / ABURTO
POINT-BLANK PAINTBALL
SPORTS FICTION
Sports Illustrated KIDS
GRAPHIC NOVELS

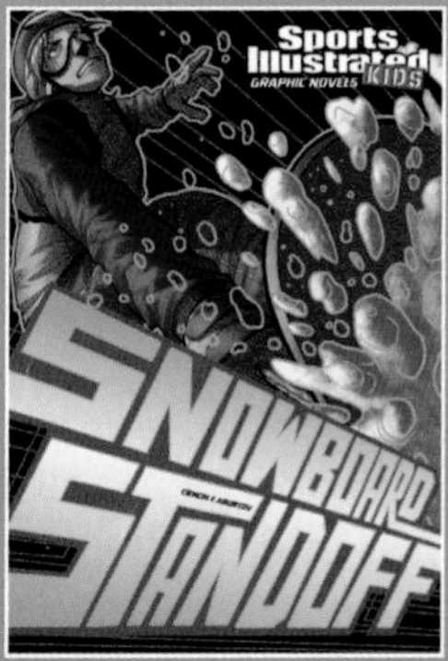
Sports Illustrated KIDS
GRAPHIC NOVELS
SNOWBOARD STANDOFF

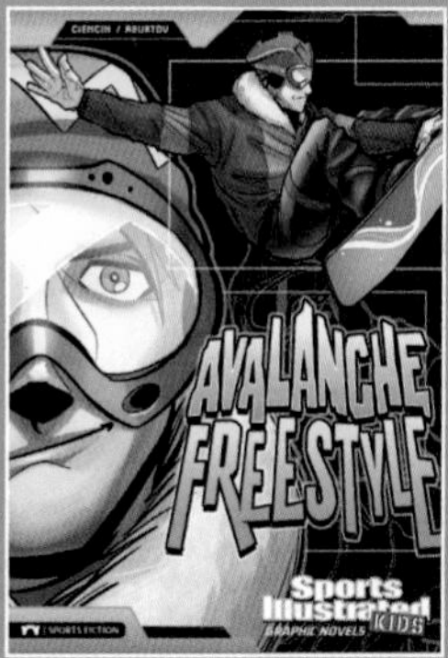
AVALANCHE FREESTYLE
Sports Illustrated KIDS
GRAPHIC NOVELS
SPORTS FICTION

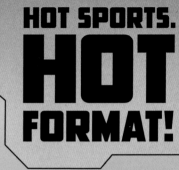

GREAT CHARACTERS BATTLE FOR SPORTS GLORY IN TODAY'S HOTTEST FORMAT–GRAPHIC NOVELS!

NLY FROM ***STONE ARCH BOOKS***

Sports Illustrated

GRAP

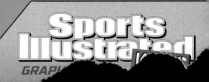

THE FUN
DOESN'T STOP
HERE!

FIND MORE
GAMES
PUZZLES
CHARACTERS

www.capstonekids.com

Still want MORE? Find cool websites and more books lik this one at www.Facthound.com. Just type in the Book I 9781434222381 and you're ready to go!

AND FOR SPORTS HEADLINES, SCORES, SI KIDS.com
STATS, PHOTOS, COOL GAMES.

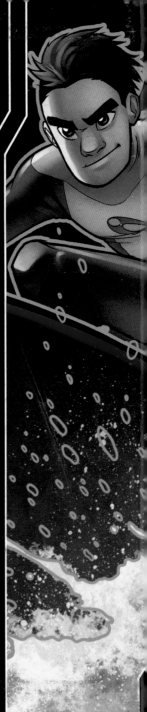